T0128253

THE NIGHT OF THE FULL MOON

OF THE

A novel set against a
WW2 BACKGROUND

GERALD GLYN WOOLLEY

authorHOUSE®

AuthorHouse™ UK
1663 Liberty Drive
Bloomington, IN 47403 USA
www.authorhouse.co.uk
Phone: UK TFN: 0800 0148641 (Toll Free inside the UK)
        UK Local: (02) 0369 56322 (+44 20 3695 6322 from outside the UK)

Published by AuthorHouse 11/17/2022

ISBN: 978-1-7283-7581-6 (sc)
ISBN: 978-1-7283-7582-3 (e)

This story is set in the first six months of June 1944 in a small town in the south of France.

While the background structure is loosely based on General Lammerding of the second SS panzer division (*Das Reich*), the notable French resistance fighter Andre Malraux, Colonel Maurice Buckmaster (leader of the French section of Special Operations Executive) and Violet Szabo, (British agent) all other names are purely imaginary.

This is a novel that depicts the personal lives of the villagers of Montauban and how they were caught up in one of the most terrifying events that traumatised France following the German occupation of 1940. The liberation of France wasn't a well-ordered sequence of events. It was a tale of factional conflicts, vicious vengeance, and reprisals – not always justified – and near anarchy in places, alongside the jubilation of freedom from occupation.

Feelings still run deep and people who lived through those times down there still don't want to talk about them. Accusations that x or y was a collaborator during the war are still muttered behind hands. There is still much guilt today in France especially about Vichy and its role in condemning so many French men and women to deportation and death. We have learned that society is only skin deep and that everyone is capable of turning on his neighbour.

As with most novels, dates and narratives have been stretched to accommodate the story line but it remains a novel, a work of fiction of human relationships, choices and fateful decisions that we today never had to face but that lead to supreme sacrifices always in the belief that personal will can triumph over evil.

COURTESY : MONTAUBAN
INFORMATION CENTRE

Montauban Town Square

CONTENTS

PREFACE

Everybody knows that the sun shines on the moon to illuminate it. When the moon is dark, the Moon is "new", and the side of the Moon facing Earth is not illuminated by the Sun. As the Moon waxes (the amount of illuminated surface as seen from Earth is increasing), the lunar phases progress through new moon, crescent moon, first-quarter moon, and full moon. The Moon is then said to wane as it passes back to new moon.

Around each new moon and full moon, the sun, Earth, and moon arrange themselves more or less along a line in space. Then the pull on the tides increases, because the gravity of the sun reinforces the moon's gravity. Thus, at new moon or full moon, the tide's range is at its maximum. This is the spring tide: the highest (and lowest) tide. Spring tides are not named for the season. This is spring in the sense of jump, burst forth, rise. So, spring tides bring the most extreme high and low tides every month, and they always happen – every month – around full and new moon.

This was the crucial reason why the Normandy landings had to go on June 6 when the high tide was at its maximum. As an Allied cross-channel invasion loomed in 1944, Rommel, convinced that it would come at high tide, installed millions of steel cement, and wooden obstacles on the possible invasion beaches, positioned so they would be under water by mid-tide. But the Allies first observed Rommel's obstacles from the air in mid-February 1944. "Thereafter they seemed to grow like mushrooms ... until by May there was an obstacle on every two or three yards of front." The obstacles came in a variety of shapes and sizes some with explosive mines on them. The Allies would certainly have liked to land at high tide, as Rommel expected, so their troops would have less beach to cross under fire. But the underwater obstacles changed that. The Allied planners now decided that initial landings must be soon after low tide so that demolition teams could blow up enough obstacles to open corridors through which the following landing craft could navigate to the beach. The tide also had to be rising, because the landing craft had to unload troops and then depart without danger of being stranded by a receding tide. There were also nontidal constraints. For secrecy, Allied forces had to cross the English Channel in darkness. But naval artillery needed about an hour of daylight to bombard the coast before the landings. Therefore, low tide had to coincide with first light, with the landings to begin one hour after. Airborne drops had to take place the night before, because the paratroopers had to land in darkness. But they also needed to see their targets, so there had to be a late-rising Moon. Only three days in June 1944 met all those requirements for "D-Day," the invasion date: 5, 6, and 7 June.

A 6-meter (18feet) tidal range meant that water would

rise at a rate of at least a meter per hour from 05:23 low tide with the beach and obstacles exposed to high tide at 10:12 am—perhaps rising even faster due to shallow-water effects. The times of low water and the speed of the tidal rise had to be known rather precisely, or there might not be enough time for the demolition teams to blow up a sufficient number of beach obstacles. Also, the low-water times were different at each of the five landing beaches (from west to east, they were code-named Utah, Omaha, Gold, Juno, and Sword). Between Utah and Sword, separated by about 100 km, the difference was more than an hour. So, H-Hour, the landing time on each beach, would have to be staggered according to the tide predictions and night of a 100% full moon

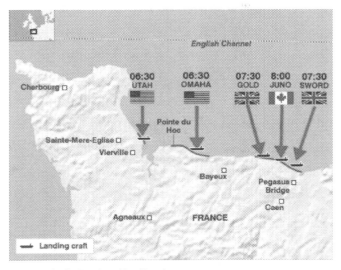

Normandy D-Day Landing Beaches

IMAGE 3 COURTESY OF CAEN HISTORY MUSEUM

MAP OF BEACHES. To show problems of tides

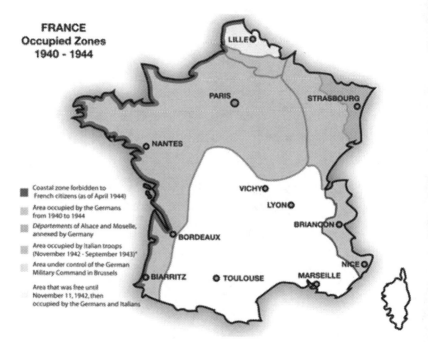

FRANCE
Occupied Zones
1940 - 1944

LILLE ⊙

PARIS ⊙

STRASBOURG ⊙

NANTES ⊙

VICHY ⊙

LYON ⊙

BRIANÇON ⊙

BORDEAUX ⊙

NICE ⊙

BIARRITZ ⊙   ⊙ TOULOUSE   MARSEILLE ⊙

■ Coastal zone forbidden to
  French citizens (as of April 1944)

  Area occupied by the Germans
  from 1940 to 1944

  Départements of Alsace and Moselle,
  annexed by Germany

  Area occupied by Italian troops
  (November 1942 - September 1943)*

  Area under control of the German
  Military Command in Brussels

  Area that was free until
  November 11, 1942, then
  occupied by the Germans and Italians

France occupied zones 1940-1944

NIGHT OF THE FULL MOON
La Nuit de la Pleine `lune

ONE
Panic

"Where is the saboteur" asked the German Officer pointing his Luger 9mm pistol at Yvette's head. She could see the lightening zig zag flashes on the mans' lapel tunic and the skull and crossbones insignia on his cap. This was the SS officer in charge of traffic movements for the *Das Reich* division in Montauban. The trembling schoolgirl smiled at him "We are just out for a cycling ride and know nothing about saboteurs or trains. He looked at her friend Terri who was older but much prettier even than Yvette with long blond hair done in pig tails making her look much younger than she was. "If you don't tell me then ten men from the town will be shot" "Even if we knew them and told you then you would probably shoot them anyway," said Terri. The SS officer glowered and summoned a soldier over and said, "take these two away and shoot them" The soldier looked aghast, much as he was a hardened veteran of the Eastern front, this was beyond his resolve. "If you do that, you will be hunted down by the allies and hung for a war crime, after all they have just landed in France. There are witnesses all around" Yvette said pointing to the French railway workers nearby desperately trying to free the axels of the low loaders with Tiger tanks aboard. "Hauptmann-Furhrer, let them go, we have much work to do and wasting lives won't get it done quicker." said the soldier. Now it was the soldiers turn to face the gun in his face. "How dare you question me?" Just then a senior officer came up. "what's going on here?" He asked. Hauptman saluted and said "Herr Oberfuhrer, these are two saboteurs who I want shot" "don't be stupid "said the SS Colonel "these are only innocent schoolgirls, and we have Americans to fight. Let's see how brave you are when we meet them." The officer holstered his pistol and soldier told them to stop the panic, to get on their bikes and vanish. Little did they know what Terri and Yvette had done during the night.

One

SOE ENGLAND

ENGLAND, 6 JANUARY 1944

Aleksander finished his supper and went to the briefing room. It was cold. It was January 1944, and Aleksander Buckingham was in the final stages of his SOE training at Beaulieu in the New Forest where he had learnt all the tradecraft associated with survival behind enemy lines in Nazi-occupied Europe. The agents were trained in planting explosives, burglary, forgery, sabotage radio operations, Morse code, and silent killing with bare hands, wire, rope, and even ordinary household items like kitchen scissors.

More unusual techniques included planting bombs inside dead rats. Other spy gadgets, now housed in the Beaulieu Museum, included a compass and map hidden in a hairbrush and a lethal blade concealed in a shoelace.

SOE, or Special Organisation Executive, was formed by Churchill in June 1940 as a clandestine army charged with "setting Europe alight" through acts of sabotage of trains, bridges, and communication installations. Sometimes, but rarely, they were charged with assassination of leading Nazi leaders. But after the murder of SS-Obergruppenfuhrer Reinhard Heydrich in Prague in May 1942, the reprisals exacted by the Germans at Lidice were regarded as too high a price to pay, and SOE activities were then more focused on a lower level. Aleksander had already done his gruelling commando training at Arisaig in Scotland and parachute training in Cheshire and by now was waiting for his first assignment. Born of a Polish father and a French mother, he was fluent in French and German. His parents had escaped first to France and then England before the war and were now living quietly in Chelmsford Essex. They knew nothing of their son's work, and he could not tell them or even hint to them at what he was doing—although his mother, like all mothers, kept anxiously prodding him for information. He had not seen them for eighteen months and was only allowed to write once a month that he was alive and well. Tonight, he was brushing up on his personal life in preparation for his meeting the next day with Maurice Buckmaster, head of F section, which handled nearly four hundred agents throughout the war. Maurice spoke French fluently so Aleksander's premonition was that the meeting would have something to do with France.

Two

MONTAUBAN

FRANCE, 6 JANUARY 1944
86 PER CENT FULL MOON

The sleepy rural town of Montauban is a commune in the Tarn-et-Garonne department in Southern France. On the border between the hills of Bas-Quercy and the rich alluvial plains of the Garonne and Tarn, there is an important road junction and busy market town. The pink bricks give the town its character typical of the region. It is the capital of the department and lies fifty kilometers (thirty-one miles) north of Toulouse. Montauban was the most populated town in Tarn-et-Garonne and the sixth most populated of Occitanic behind Toulouse, Montpellier, Nimes, Perpignan, and Béziers. The beautiful river of the Tarn with its deep gorges flows 350 kilometers to join the Garonne flowing down to Bordeaux.

Yves lived with his sister, Yvette, and their mother,

Francoise, in a little house at 2 Rue de Palisse near the centre south of the river and five minutes' walk from the railway station. Their father, Fabrice, had been captured when the French army surrendered in 1940 and was a prisoner of war in Germany. Francois only had the occasional heavily censored postcard permitted by the Germans each month to say he was well. Madelaine Bezier baked bread in the bakery next door, great big roundels almost a metre across. The owner, Jacques, had been shot by the Germans some years earlier in 1941 for trying to escape from his barn where arms were being stored. Madam Bezier always believed he had been betrayed out of spite by a woman whom he promised to marry then ditched. Madelaine assumed his role and baked every day when there was flour available. Madelaine was a good-looking woman in her early thirties, maybe even beautiful some would say. Yves, 16, helped in the local garage while his elder sister, 19, helped in the local infant school and the hospital. Life had been quiet in this corner of France; the Germans were polite and paid for their food and did nothing to trouble them—they left that to the Gendarmes and the dreaded Milice, a political organisation created in 1943 by Marshall Petain to help combat the growing resistance movements. Montauban was in the zone libre, or demilitarised zone, under control by the Vichy regime, so the area was relatively quiet so that the Germans could free up their panzer divisions for the invasion of Russia. Marechal Petain placed in charge of Vichy was doing the Germans' dirty work and was far more brutal to his own Frenchman than were the Germans. He introduced the laws against the Jews just after the Germans invaded.

from Montauban down to Toulouse and north to Brive. He was also responsible for doing all the shunting in the sidings and sorting out the train timetables; there were four BR52 2-10-0 steam locomotives in the sidings, two of them kept continuously in steam in case others broke down and were needed by the military. This locomotive was the workhorse of the German and French railways, built with solder instead of rivets to save weight, and over six thousand were made. Hans, his German guard, and Raoul were on a reserve list so, as such, had not been sent away to Germany, but he knew everything that was going on with regard to traffic movements and the German military. Paul told Yves that nothing extraordinary was happening; the Germans had arrived by road and there were no train movements on the timetable. "Everybody must remain calm," said Paul. "And I'm sure that if anything is going to happen, my father will know it before anybody

YVETTE AND PASCAL

Yvette was Yves sister and liked playing the piano, she was quite well advanced for her age taking lessons every week from Maria who lived a few houses away in the same street; she could play quite well and often she was practicing and playing traditional old French songs but also Chopin and Beethoven despite the disapproval of her teacher who said that she should not be playing anything German at this time but she was a plucky if stubborn little girl and didn't see why it should spoil her past-time; she was also in love there was a boy in the village called Pascal who was 20 years of age and worked on a farm near Montauban as a cowherd and raising chickens for sale in the market often to the black market but one could not be choosy at this time; most of his production of cattle, pigs and sheep had been confiscated by the Vichy French and latterly by the Germans when they came to the town. They left him with two dozen chickens, and their eggs. There was also a magnificent rooster with long golden plumage. Whenever Yvette visited, she loved the song of the rooster, strident, full of hope and promise of life to come. Pascal often rode into town bringing with him a spare pony for a Yvette and they rode out into the countryside to his farm 2 km away. the farm was situated on a rising slope with a stream running through it and heavily wooded areas of the trails and trees to ride through. Yvette had known Pascal for about six months before he stopped going to school because there was no point in him taking any more education; there is no college or university to go to anyway; he liked his daily life on the farm, and he saw that one day he will inherit the farm and his parents were now in their late 50s early 60s. They still lived on the farm but let Pascal manage it. After all there was nothing much left to manage. After their days riding Yvette would smuggle back into town vegetables and fresh potatoes and onions everything needed in the kitchen to at least make good soup together with the bread next door from the bakery meant that they never went hungry although they missed some of the meat that they used to have before

"what do you think is going to happen" Yvette's had said to Pascal one evening.

"all the young men have been sent away and I don't want that to happen to you"

"don't worry, the Germans or the Vichy French won't touch me because I supply them with chickens and besides I am from Alsace, which is more Germany than France, well at least right now."

"well, I would hate to see you be taken away because I have strong feelings for you and I hope after the war whenever that might be we get closer together, marry and raise a family"

"ha ha" said Pascal "you are quite the little homemaker, I'm not ready to settle down yet it'll take a long time to get the farm back into production before I even think about asking you to marry me. I only have two goats left but they will be good for a feast at Easter time when we can have the special traditional goat's dinner".

Pascal also only had two horses left, one young mare of about 13 or 14 hands and the other was a young pony. The Germans had taken all the old dray horses back in 1942 when they invaded Russia because the Wehrmacht was still largely a horse drawn army and there were no replacements available, but Yvette liked to ride the pony with him to the woods. One day they went for a picnic down to the small stream. This being January it was still frosty and icy, so the going was slow, and they had to take heavy coats and rugs. Pascal had brought with him rugs to lie on, a cooked chicken and Yvette brought some bread which provided a wonderful lunch beside a drinking stream. Yvette was dressed in a sensible knee length black skirt, white blouse under grey wool coat and had resisted all amorous advances from Pascal but she allowed him to stroke her stomach but as soon as his hand strayed down her skirt to the sticky regions and forbidden area which aroused her more than she could ever have known, and she pulled she pulled his hand away scared as she was not to get pregnant and to save herself from when her father returned to give her away. Her father was the man in her life, and she missed him terribly and Pascal had a adopted a father figure towards her of which she was immensely proud.

She had never known such strong feelings of now wanting to be protected and respected by Pascal and grow a life together. She ached with longingness for his company; to live on his farm and re-stock with animals and ponies whose stable yard smell and warmth she adored as the scent of life. Where did this yearning, and aching come from? Where were its roots and why did it infuse her whole body with a desire to possess something of her own? Love was too simple a word for it, that word was used by silly girls at school who had girlish infatuations with the sexually aggressive young boys in class. No, this was a stronger primeval feeling, wanting to be safe, guarded and protected.

Yvette was a striking girl of 19 the shoulder length dark brown hair and a strong young body with an hourglass figure and voluptuous legs and curvy thighs. her breasts were not that well-developed, but she was very homely girl now in her late teens just right for motherhood. Pascal knew also that he was in love with her, and it annoyed him when she played with her glossy brown hair twirling it and then because he wanted to stroke it and she left him and was content to align with her head on his stomach under the shade of the trees through which the weak January sun struggled to filter with dabbling spots of light, beside the little stream with the ponies grazing nearby. he knew he had to wait, and all would be alright in the end but who knew when the end would be. He teased her calling her his 'ittle cuckoo.'

Why do you call me that?' asked Yvette.

"well because you want to drop your nest into my life, you are quite the little homemaker. But regard it as a term of endearment' he said.

Her mother knew all about her little horse rides out with Pascal and continuously stressed to her that now is not the time for her to get it herself into any trouble; while she often resented her mother giving her advice like any daughter mother relationship, she knew she was right, and she obeyed. Her mother constantly reminded her that she held the future of France in her tummy with babies waiting to be born and the day would come when it would, by a miracle of nature, come true.

"So, tell me Pascal, there are rumours that you hide weapons on your farm for the Maquis -is it true?" "Certainly not, that would get us all shot. Once we helped a Jewish family to hide but they moved on". Pascal sighed, "we could have been deported for that". Pascal was built with a strong torso, blond hair and blue eyes as his family were originally from Alsace and maybe their roots were of some German ancestry. He had brought with him pieces of air- dried ham that he saved from the last time the farm had pigs. He unwrapped it and held it up to her nose to smell. Her little nostrils flared and twitched like a young doe in the forest sniffing lichen. "Wow that smells so good. It's been a long time since I tasted this". As the daylight hours were short Pascal and Yvette returned to the farm about 4 pm stabled the horses and then Yvette walked the 2 kilometers back to Montauban, carrying a small sack of potatoes.

"Yvette," said her mother, go around to Madelaine next door, give her some potatoes and ask if she has a baguette spare." Yvette knocked on the door – Madam Bezier opened it and said "Hello Yvette, come in. Oh, you've brought me some potatoes, how very kind."

'I was wondering madam if you have a baguette left over from this morning, please? "Well, I do but it's a bit stale already, 'don't worry said Yvette it's just for some soup. Of course, Yvette, any time,' said Madelaine. Yvette looked at her with her long dark hair hanging onto her shoulders. 'May I ask Madam a personal question? Why have you not taken another man in your life, you are still young and very pretty?"

'Aha, what a big question. You shouldn't be asking that sort of thing at your age but there are many reasons; my husband only died three years ago so it's a bit early for that and if the war ends this year there will be lots of men returning from Germany."

"Are there men in the village you like?" asked Yvette innocently.

"Not to the extent that I want to share my bed let alone my bread recipe with! who knows running off with that would be worse than running out on me, so I have time to choose carefully. I am sure the men in this village play around sometimes," she said with a little twinkle in

12

her eye. "it's a French habit, the art of seduction. I can never remember a divorce due to so called infidelity. If one is tired of one's husband then a little bit of spice will make him even more attractive to you and it's never too late",

"My teacher says it's a bit late if you leave decisions too long,' said Yvette. "Well, said Madelaine, let's put it this way – where would I find a good strong handsome young boy like your Pascal? "Yvette blushed deeply. "I didn't know you knew about Pascal said Yvette. "I think there is no one in the town that doesn't,' said Madelaine.

Yvette took the baguette and hurried back home. that night was the usual potato, onion and carrot soup with the once fresh bread. No meat was available, and Yvette felt guilty for gorging herself on chicken at lunch time with Pascal; then after supper she played a little on the piano practicing her scales attempting a piece from Beethoven. She loved Beethoven but wished she could play better. It was alright having lessons from old Madam Maria in the village, but the lessons lacked excitement and passion. Besides Maria smelled.

Three

PASCAL'S NIGHT -TIME ADVENTURE

JANUARY 7TH

Later the next night Pascal left the farm with ten friends carrying antiquated firearms; shotguns and an old rifle or two and made their way 10 miles into the uplands of the countryside. It was by now 1 AM and time for their meeting with the local maquis to receive a parachute drop of arms from England. it was cold; they sat themselves around as best as possible and then at the appointed hour of 2 AM they turned on their torches in an arrow format, two men down the centre and four down each side in a large deserted field surrounded by dense forest and trees. this was the most dangerous time but always quiet it was almost the night of the full moon after all and although it wasn't completely full at 94% it was all that was needed for the plane to find them over the dropping zone nothing happened for half an hour. They turned their torches off to save power, batteries were very expensive and extremely difficult to acquire. then one of the men heard a low growling in the sky. They turned the torches on again and soon coming overhead like a giant Eagle wafting the breeze away from them was an RAF plane, it circled and came back in very low and then released parachutes holding boxes of cargo at 200 feet. Then it was gone. How Pascal wished he could be on the plane. The job was then to untangle parachutes and bury them. But the three canisters were heavy and not able to be carried on their own so the men had brought sacks and bags to pack the grenades ammunition and cigarettes. The cannisters were covered in bracken. They extracted with great sense of excitement the mills bombes, grenades, TNT explosive and ammunition for the 6 Sten guns wrapped in oily waxed paper and finally the cigarettes. By this time, it was 4: 30 in the morning they were all exhausted but they managed to cover the 10 km back to the Farm without mishap and there underneath the straw in the barn were floor boards which they opened up and lowered all the delivery into a large pit lined with sacking which they had previously prepared then covered it over with straw and nailed the boards down again and covered them all with huge stacks of hay. Pascal crept into bed and slept until he was awoken by his father saying: "Pascal, its seven o'clock and we have got to get on with a day's work" this is it how it went; sometimes planes never arrived as promised so the journey was futile. other times they did not bring anything on any substance just a few handguns and grenades, but they all have a sense that they are building up reserves for when they day came, and the Maquis would breakout and help fight the enemy.

The next night was the same: only six Sten guns and some TNT, Very disappointing. By now they were all exhausted. Pascal slept in the hay. he was rudely awoken again by his father saying: Pascal we got to get on with a day's work. Why are you sleeping so much? Are you up to something dangerous? this is it how it went on: sometimes planes did not arrive, so the journey was futile other times it only brings nothing of any substance just a few handguns.

This was the first-time pascals farm had been chosen for an ammunition dump. his parents knew nothing about it. Pascal had been contacted by the Maquis and asked if he would help. He knew the dangers but thought that with the current German activity in the area which was very small that the risk had to be taken. he had met the set of friends all from farms around all intent on helping. one of the farms had a radio set operated he was told by a young girl maybe she was French maybe she wasn't French but nevertheless this is how they were in contact with London sending personal messages like "Antoine has a fat pig. All the Lavender is no good this year". all these messages meant something to the various people. They were called personal messages which London broadcast to the resistance, often they would be a warning for somebody not to go to a particular place the next day or next week. a lot of lives have been saved that way because of the forewarning to other people who were being hunted by the Gendarmes.

Four

COOLING OFF

JANUARY 10

Pascal decided to cool his relationship with `Yvette. He didn't want to involve her in something if it went wrong. She would be miffed and think that he was brushing her off. This was exactly what Yvette began to think as no messages of invitations to Farm came. And Yvette pined for her boyfriend – not unnoticed by the other girls at school or by her mother who sensed something was wrong.

"Don't worry" said Yves suddenly feeling important that he could solve the mystery of his sister's dejectedness, "its boy trouble" he said gleefully. "which boy, is it a boy in class" asked his mother when Yves kept prodding the question mischievously. Francoise confronted Yvette

"why are you so mopey? Has someone or something upset you? To be honest Francoise had noticed that supply of potatoes and eggs had dried up. "It's Pascal' she replied, "he doesn't love me anymore. No message has come from

17

him for a week now." Her mother sat her down "It's not good for you to be emotionally entangled at your age and from what I hear Pascal has been involved with the Maquis which is highly dangerous." That's all lies pouted Yvette with tears in her eyes, who told you that" Just a rumour said her mother. Now go and do some piano practice, you haven't done any this week. Yvette felt like exploding; she bared her teeth and uttered a growl, but she knew her mother was trying to do the best for them and so swallowed her pride. She went and hit the ivories with resounding anger in her fingers. She was confused. Pascal had never said anything to her about the Maquis. Who were they anyway and what did they want with Pascal? The next day she decided to speak to Raoul's son Paul at school about if he knew anything he wasn't telling.

"My fathers' got a difficult enough job with the railway for him to get involved with anything and if he doesn't tell me then I don't know anything."

RAOUL AND HANS

The Germans had long settled down into their guard duties, what a posting to this quiet area of France with its good wine and food. Most of them were over 50 years of age and had been drawn from active service last year to serve as guards. They didn't cause the townsfolk any problems, unlike the Gendarmes and the Milice who seemed to be enjoying the persecution of their French citizens and settling old scores. Raoul had a guard in his signal box with him all day long and until 10pm at night when the last train arrived from Toulouse. Normally the same soldier Hans every day. Hans had never been married and was from Stuttgart, the city was being heavily bombed to destroy the ball bearings factories. He hadn't been back home for 3 years, and he and Raoul got on well, same age at 48 and shared stories of the First World War and women they had known. Hans always managed to bring a bottle of Schnapps with him which during the cold winter nights was most welcome. It was from Hans that Raoul got all his information of what was happening with the German Army, sometimes it proved lifesaving as Hans would tell Raoul to make sure his family were not out on the streets on certain nights when the Germans made a sweep, picking up young men for work in Germany.

"But you know Raoul, we could never have done any of these things without the help of the French, especially the Gendarmes with their local knowledge" he said. "I have never known a people who betrayed each other so much as the French; even in Poland or Hungary where I was at the start of the war, they all held together" Raoul said nothing. Hans continued "but for living out the war France is the best." Raoul agreed and said "Hans, war does strange things to people – they become monsters"

"So, you know the war is ending," said Hans, "the allied invasion is coming, and Germany will be completely defeated. Devastated. But there is talk of new super weapons that will save us and win the war. That is probably true because Hitler has always backed technology and invested in new ideas. We are told that it's our duty to save France from the English and Americans.

But why bother I say? France can save itself. Its Germany that needs to be saved from the Russians"

"Do you want to be saved or would you rather surrender and then go home and live a peaceful life? You have a choice," Said Raoul. Hans said nothing. He realised that such talk could get him into trouble.

"Aren't you a bit old for the army Hans" asked Raoul. "Ache, nine, there is no more army left so Hitler is asking for old men and young boys to help defend the Fatherland. I once almost wanted to join the Hitler Youth, but of course was too old. Anyway, that was a cult organisation built up for political and military ends; never has a generation been so completely taken over by a totalitarian state and so thoroughly brainwashed. Children the age of 10 joined the Junvolk movement, at 14 they joined the Hitler youth, and at 18 they joined the party, the Wehrmacht the SA or the SS. Religion was cast aside, the only real science taught in schools was physics, and it was a tough military style education, breeding them for hardship and battle, with the promise that one day they could be a Gaulieter of Bavaria or Minsk. But no one could escape the excitement of the massed drums, torch lit rallies, the singing of the fahne Hoch; it was mesmeric. All the boys and girls wanted to join. They were given uniforms and little rucksacks. I was already 35 years old and, in a reserve, occupation making bigger army rucksacks. I was lucky to have missed the fanatical crusade that followed; no surrender; death is more honourable. Like Teutonic knights of old'

"So, where did it start unravelling?" asked Raoul.

"The big mistake Hitler made was to voluntarily

declare war on the USA while still fighting in Russia. You didn't need to be a professor to see that was stupid. In Russia Germany very nearly won despite the huge distances but the USA could never have been invaded and Hitler had no idea of the huge mass production capabilities of the USA. Also, it wasn't Ivan who really defeated us; it was the cold, the terrible cold weather killed the troops, the horses and the equipment. Neither did Hitler imagine the 'Lend Lease' between the Americans and the Russians, the USA has kept Russia supplied with trucks, tanks, supplies and planes. Sent in precious convoys to England and then ten per cent were sent on to Russia trough the artic. That was 11 December 1941. I was in the hospital for a minor problem before being sent down here. Now, anyone who can fire a panzerfaust (grenade launcher) is sent to the East to try and stop the Russian tanks. We have no choice. There is no surrender only total war and total destruction. We have probably lost 80% of all our menfolk in Russia."

They had another sip of schnapps together; the last train arrived hissing and puffing into the station and screeched to a halt. A few soldiers and old men got off and disappeared into the darkness. Raoul pulled various levers and threw all signals to red, dead stop. Then they locked up and left.

Five

MISSION BRIEFING

ENGLAND, MONDAY JANUARY 17TH

Aleksander's meeting with Maurice Buckmaster, the head of F section at 64 Baker Street, the HQ of the SOE (special operations executive) and a fitting address for sleuths being also the street address of Sherlock Holmes. SOE was sometimes referred to as "The baker Street Irregulars" or Churchills secret army. Founded in 1942 by Churchill to set Europe alight it was responsible for all clandestine operations in occupied Europe. He was slightly early but waited outside in the corridor although Maurice knew he was already there. Then at 10 am promptly the door opened, and he was waved inside a somewhat dim and dark room by the secretary … The room was very plain, with a desk, two chairs and a single bare lightbulb. Maurice was sitting on one of the chairs and motioned him to sit down. There was a thin dossier on the table which Maurice opened. He then began asking Aleksander about his background and upbringing.

Aleksander had no idea what was going to be discussed. About half-way through the interview Maurice suddenly, in mid-sentence, switched to French and continued as if nothing had happened. It was a favourite trick to snare those who were not fluent. Aleksander took it in his stride and answered everything, discussed everything and conversed with Maurice in deep French slang and language of the street with a touch of a Marseilles accent. Finally, after two hours Maurice said that he wanted Aleksander to go to South of France, to co-ordinate the activities of the five resistance movements in and around the Dordogne and the village of Montauban near Toulouse. His mission was to try and get the resistance chiefs to listen, to stop squabbling amongst themselves and to report on any increased or unusual activity. At the moment Maurice said, "the area is still recovering from the disaster of April 1943 when one key resistance circuit called PRUNUS was infiltrated by the Abwher (German counter intelligence) and at least six of our best agents were rounded up and executed, so while it's still pretty sleepy down there from a military viewpoint, the Gestapo are very active trying to break the last circuit called PIMENTO and the chief of Gestapo in Lyon, Claus Barbie, has been wreaking havoc over the last few years in infiltrating our circuits. We have made lots of mistakes and one of them was not to have enough radios; one goes down and it destroys the whole network so you will have a radio operator with you. Also, we now have a good man in charge there called Tony, so we do not want another debacle like last year. So, you have to build a new circuit from the ground up, don't trust any existing so called senior people in local government, many are working very closely with the Vichy administration out of a reluctant need to protect their families and will give anyone away. We have received rumours from Switzerland via our Lyon circuit that the Germans may be moving more troops to the south in the belief that the allies will land there, and your mission is to look listen and report."

"No heroics, just observation. Do not encourage the mass up-rising of the French- there will be terrible reprisals. They will never win in open battle against the Germans. Just encourage the slow evolution of specifically targeted operations. Your code name is "Claude Monet" – you are a wine merchant from Bordeaux. Your history is all here, forget Aleksander, its far too polish, learn everything about Claude. You will have a radio operator, Jenny, to go with you. Radios are very scarce in France now because of the Gestapo capturing the operators so be careful. We only have six in the whole of France with four having contact to London". He was given the code names of other British agents in the area, three of them in Bordeaux, Montpellier and Carcassone. Jenny will also have a code name "Petite Chitigones -Little Rascal". Help each other to learn your new identities. There will be a poem 48 hours before D day the first half being 'Wound my heart' – to be followed by the second line the day before and then the night before there will be 2 coded messages – one specifically for you "La nuit de la plaine lune" – this will signal the invasion is imminent. Then 'It is hot in Cairo' – that will be your first personal message 24 hours before for the maquis in your area to rise with tactical road, rail and communications sabotage — remember no extremes especially shooting German officers — that will cause unnecessary reprisals. Now you are going to be lucky; no parachuting — we will use a long -range Lysander because of Jenny, the new heavier radio and we want to extract one of our agents from there back to England".

Aleksander, now Claude in his new identity, was happy about the no parachuting — the type "A" had a bad habit of corkscrewing and tangling everything up. Then the meeting was over, and Claude was told to report to RAF operations at Tempsford. RAF Tempsford, a Royal Air Force station located 2.3 miles northeast of Sandy, Bedfordshire, England and 4.4 miles south of St. Neots, Cambridgeshire, England. As part of the Royal Air Force Special Duty Service, the airfield was perhaps the most secret airfield of the Second World War

JENNY

The next day he met Jenny, an ordinary looking girl in her mid-twenties and French by birth form Paris. Although fairly plain she was very tough, and the best shot of the whole training group. The final briefing consisted of a full change of clothes with no English labels or bus ticket stubs in the pockets, French identity and ration cards, the latest travel pass and permits, money, emergency rations, maps, compass, service revolver and a pen in the top of which was a small tube in which was the pill of last resort should he be captured. 'When would they go?' Jenny asked him.

"That's not for us to know — we will be given 8

hours -notice – it could be any night from now on, so we just have to wait. We won't be allowed out of the base now, so we have to make the most of it." They were to focus on their training and keeping fit with daily runs around the camp and a Sargent major who made their lives hell, but they knew that they had to be super fit. The cinema at the camp helped pass the time with old films and newsreels but the days went by with monotony and anti-climax. The rest of January dragged by into early February until the night of February 6th.

Six

TWO EGGS ON MY PLATE

SUNDAY FEBRUARY 6, 1944. 94% FULL MOON. WEATHER 12C AND CLOUDY

That night dinner was special – ham and two eggs with plenty of each. "Aha" said Claude "Two eggs on my plate, this is the night we go" Sure enough at 7pm they were told to report to the operations room where final briefings were given. The take-off will be at 1130 tonight. It's a very full moon which is perfect. The Lysander needed an almost full moon to fly by to aid navigation. "You will arrive at about 2.30 am. The Lysander can land in a very short space, about 100 yards. You will have to be out the aircraft in 10 seconds; packages will follow, then two people will get in and the whole operation from landing until take off is one minute. You will be met by our contact, code name "Le Rat Rouge" and be taken to a safe house." Stomach muscles tightened but now the sooner the better thought Claude.

At 11pm they gathered on the airfield. It was raining but the weather reports for France were good, some low cloud but mainly dry and clear. The distance of 418 miles and back was too far for the standard fuel tank of 106 gallons, so a long-range extra gallon tank was hung underneath with another 150 gallons. This, with the new Mk 111 design and supercharged Bristol Perseus 12 valve radial piston engine enabled a round trip to Limoges area and back at 212 mph flying at 15,000 feet. They climbed on board up the permanent ladder into the cramped fuselage. Pilot, navigator plus the two passengers and gear plus the extra fuel took up most of the 1,000-net payload. The huge single engine Bristol Mercury with 3 bladed props began to turn and slowly the "Little Lizzie" plane (as she was known) taxied to the edge of the grass strip. With the brakes fully on, the pilot powered up to maximum revs then let go the brakes. It only needed 100 yards to get airborne and they were away up into the black sky climbing hard. Suddenly the Channel shimmered below them in the moonlight then was gone behind cloud. This was helpful to avoid the flak that came up into them in sheets of fire and puffs once over Normandy. Then it was quiet except for the wind and the engine. Their heading was almost due south to map co-ordinates 44.12N. 1.29W an open field in the uplands North of Montastruc, a small hamlet a few miles northeast of Toulouse in the department of Haut-Garonne, one of the many drop zone sites the Maquis used. Claude snoozed as the drone of the engine lulled him dozy; Jenny was quiet but wide awake. "Ten minutes to destination," said the pilot. Then the plane was diving sharply to an arrow of light below them and levelled out just seconds before the wheels hit the ground and rough grassy bumpy field which the Lysanders tough undercarriage construction coped with well. The plane came to a stop, door thrown open, Claude and Jenny hustled out throwing their baggage to the ground, two men got on and the Lysander then revved, turned and took off. "One minute 10 seconds" said the pilot, getting better.

A man approached Claude and shook his hand; he was dressed in black dungarees, heavy sweater covered with a military type of grey jacket and black berry. "Je suis Le Rat" he said and then gave Jenny a hug. "Quick, my men will carry the baggage; we must now walk for about an hour to your base." Le Rat led them, and three other men armed with Sten guns, and the rest of the reception team dissolved into the night. It seemed a long walk but after an hour and a bit they arrived at a dark farmhouse situated on rising ground with thick woods at the back. Le Rat knocked three times then another one knock. A voice asked, "who is there?'

The answer and password 'Fromage blanc' came and the door was opened by the shepherd who acknowledged Le Rat with a kiss and hug. Le Rat then spoke to Claude and Jenny. Today we stay here, and we will move on tonight to your safe house outside Montauban. 'How far is that' asked Claude? 'About 50 kilometers from here but we will have transport and go by the back roads.' Claude and Jenny were exhausted and flopped down on the straw mattresses on the floor, falling directly asleep. About four hours later they were awakened by goats nibbling at the straw they were lying on. Jenny could smell all the animal smells. She got up slowly, yawned and stretched. Claude rose and patted himself down, brushing straw down that seemed to have stuck everywhere. They were offered coffee, with a very strange flavour. 'Sorry' said Le Rat 'it's made from acorns; we haven't had real coffee for years, but it's hot'

Bread with butter and an apple followed. Now it was nearly noon. It was raining. They gathered their luggage and with a bottle of spring water clutched in their hands, they got into the little Citroen van. It looked so funny with its corrugated sides and small thin wheels. It was hardly any better than a motorcycle in a tin shed thought Jenny and the little sewing machine engine put putted into life. They trundled off down the road through the woods and arrived two hours later at a farmhouse set high above the town of Montauban down in the valley. It all looked so peaceful, difficult to believe that enemy soldiers and danger were not far away, thought Jenny

FEBRUARY 7TH

The door was opened by Madam Le Grange surrounded by two sheep dogs and an Alsatian, who hustled them inside into a kitchen lit by a single oil lamp. There was a wonderful smell of cooking from the furnace, a huge- blackened fireplace set into the white- washed walls in which numerous pots and pans sat on the sides and dominate by the large spit upon which hung what looked like a whole wild boar, turning and sizzling slowly. The dogs stretched out in front of the fire anxious for any morsels that might drop their way. "Hello, my name is

Madam Le Grange, and you are safe here. No Germans for about ten miles near Montauban, so sit and have some soup" They sat at a rough-hewn old oak table in front of the fire that gradually warmed them all through. Apart from the soup there was cold rabbit meat and thick chunky bread with a firm mellow mountain sheep's milk cheese. A jug of cider was handed round.

They ate in silence then Le Rat was the first to speak. "In the morning before first light me and my men will be gone back to our homes. Upstairs you will find two bedrooms, one for Messieurs and one for Madam. Have a good rest and we will meet again in two days. I will come here. If you need anything Madam Le Grange will get in touch with me. We keep our communication network very short to protect the circuit. Remember if you are transmitting, keep it very short and stop after five minutes. The Germans have a habit of shutting off the power to try and track users in the night. "Dormez bien" and with that Le Rat and his men left with their newly acquired Sten guns and grenades. Madam Le Grange was a plump lady with a huge warm smile and in her mid-thirties. Her hair was white and trussed at the back and over her head as though she had tied much longer hair together in plats and then tied and pinned it into her hair. Claude asked about the huge boar cooking over the fire "Do you have a large family to feed" he asked. "Ah my family is now all the maquisards living in the hills. They hunted and shot the boar yesterday —there are many in the woods. my husband is a prisoner of war and my daughters both live in Montauban; they were happily married at a young age, and both have baby-boys, so I am a very lucky grandmother. Fortunately, their husbands work in the Abattoir – not a terribly nice occupation but for the moment it is safe. The Germans must have their supply of pig-meat, so they are regarded as essential to the war effort." Claude told her all about England and how the bombing had stopped over a year ago, so the people and the country were happy to see signs of the war ending. The only threat still comes from the doodle bugs and U Boats – they are still sinking our supply ships but even they are on the losing side now with more and more being sunk by planes and convoy destroyers." Jenny said nothing and Claude could see her eyes closing. "To bed and thank you for the food and your welcome" Claude said. "if you ever get back to England and then return to here," Madam la Grange said, "bring us some DDT. The Germans have banned it as it could be used for explosives but for us, we need it to kill the bed bugs". With that they all retired for what was left of the night. Despite the cockerel crowing at dawn and the bed bugs, they both slept on until mid-morning and awoke to a crisp cold day with frost on the ground glinting in the pale morning light. But at least the rain had stopped.

Seven

BROKEN EGGS

Yvette liked the days that were quietly lengthening, it brought hope from the dark days of December. While the nights were cold at 3 degree C, the sun at midday brought 10-12c and was warm. She still had no message from Pascal at the farm and was resigned to her daily routine of school and homework. Her mother was more relaxed about the relationship Yves had with Pascal, beginning to believe that the smouldering embers of infatuation and puppy love were slowly dying, or at least not glowing so red. But she was mistaken. At supper that evening she raised the subject over the dinner of sausages and pickled cabbage. "Ma, can I go up to the farm and get some eggs today?' Her mother knew this was an excuse to see Pascal, but she relented. After all Yvette was 19 and a young woman'. Yes, but take care and be straight back. Try and get enough for Madam Spiral next door who does the washing for us."

With that Yvette left the house to go to the farm. Then she saw Paul, Yves friend. "Where are you going? He asked. "None of your business, why? "she replied. "Well, you must be careful, I heard my father say that the Germans are going to do one of the regular sweeps today"

"Well, they won't sweep me, I know the back trails and little roads"

"Ah you are going to see Pascal at the farm then. That is dangerous"

Yvette bit her lip, how foolish to let Paul know her intentions. But her love for Pascal was strong and drove her onward at a quicker pace, and without turning her head back she was gone up the road. It normally took an hour of walking to get to the farm but today she was careful to avoid the normal main road, so it was nearly an hour and a half later at 11am that she came in sight of the farm. All looked normal, the cockerel was in full voice, striding around pecking here and there around his hens; that and the sound of sheep mewing in the fields were safe comforting noises. Then she saw Pascal chopping wood and stacking a huge pile. His back was towards her, wearing only a tee shirt. she slowly moved forward savouring every ripple showing in his back as he swung the axe. She could see his shirt was drenched with sweat which made him all the more appealing, animal like. Her heart leapt and started pounding in her breast. "Hi Pascal, it's me Yvette" she shouted. Pascal stopped and turned with his big smile beaming radiating out like a single ray from the sun. He looked even more handsome than she remembered, bigger, stronger and gorgeous blond dishevelled hair falling in locks down to his shoulder.

"Yvette's, how are you? Its lovely to see you again" he came forward and gave her a kiss on each cheek. Yvette threw her arms around him and squeezed. She felt his warmth surge within her "Hey, hang on, go easy" he said, "I'm not dressed to receive such a pretty girl!" This only made him more desirable, and she felt her fingers walking down his thigh. He pulled away.

"Yvette, what are you doing here" he said gently with no reproach but firm enough for her to suddenly think. "Well, it's been so long since I was with you, over a month. Do you remember the day we had a pick-nick in the forest? I'm sure the flowers are well out now and I was hoping we might go back to that magic spot."

"Yvette, you have to listen. The Germans are becoming more active now with their patrols. A month ago, they never came here but the increased activity of the Maquis further towards Tulle has had an effect. Now there is a patrol every few days; not that they do anything, I think it's just to prove to their commanders that they are active and not sleeping all day. I heard that there are now over 3,000 maquisards commissioned by the Francs-Tireurs and Partisans FTP who are evading the compulsory STO or ("Service de Travail Obligatoire"). They have taken to the hills and caves of the Correze department and the Dordogne. The Germans don't have enough men to catch them, so they are fed by local famers and go and collect arms drops from the parachuting deliveries. Everything is pretty normal apart from that. But the point is you mustn't be caught out of curfew, or give them any cause for further investigation"

Yvette listened in silence and picked up one of the

small, chopped logs. She sniffed the pine bark, smelt the wild forest in a single inhalation and fingered the rough tactile texture of the white layered inside, thinking how wonderful nature was to create a tree maybe 100 years old. Then replied with a girlish pout. "Pascal, this log will keep you warm but not as warm as my love for you, which will burn brighter and longer but" she paused "maybe you don't you love me any-more?"

Pascal said nothing. "Ma said she heard rumours of you being involved with the partisans, is that true?" She spoke.

"You know I can't talk about that. And yes, I love you but for that very reason I want you to stop coming here until it's all over"

"When will that be? It seems like it will never be over." She quipped. I walked a long way to see you Pascal, can I have some water?"

"Let's go inside and have a drink' he said.

The kitchen, like most farmhouses was the living space for humans and animals alike. The log fire was burning brightly and made the room cosy. Paul fetched an earthenware jug and poured out two glasses of cold mountain stream water. "Wow that's so good," said Yvette. "Nothing like fresh mountain spring water," said Pascal. "Where are your parents' said Yvette? They went for a long walk up the hill to pick mushroom and nuts." Together they sat for a while then Yvette said "Pascal, do you have any spare eggs please? We could use some".

"Yes of course" he said almost pleased to change the subject. He went into the scullery and brought out a basket of eggs all laid down in straw. "Some are fresh today, feel them. They are still warm" Yvette felt the eggs, and the gentle heat made her sigh "That's life in there, your little brood are laying well." She picked out six and put them in her satchel. She would have liked a dozen but there weren't enough there for that.

"Now, sorry to say but I have got to finish the logs and then I must feed and clean the ponies" he said.

"Can I help?" She asked earnestly. "Not today, you would only distract me." He said. After a few minutes silence she stood up and made for the door without saying another word. Somehow something inside her had died a little; it was like someone pulling down trellis of roses over her back door at home; a pin prick of sharpness and the beauty all gone. She felt gutted and deflated, like the bath bubbles she blew up into the air that were happy bubbles and then they died. But bubbles could be replaced over and over. Except this little bubble that had burst in her heart felt like all the bubbles in eternity. Why was he being so cold?

"It will be over soon, there's only one way ahead and that is for France to be free again" he said.

She half turned and gave him a weak smile but said nothing.

About twenty minutes away from the farm she decided to follow the main road again. It was just before a corner that she heard the noise. Engines and rattling sounds of tracked vehicles. She looked around for cover. There was none. She decided to run for the woods about fifty meters away up a hill. She sprinted as fast as she could and without thinking dived into the thickets falling heavily onto the muddy ground on her satchel. She poked her head out from behind the tree as the lead vehicle came around the corner. It was the usual BMW R71 heavy motorcycle with side car combination and MG34 machine gun. Behind was the lightly armoured half–track packing an MG42 machine gun with ten soldiers in. This standard German fire power unit could provide reconnaissance duties and suppressing fire against an enemy. Partisans would stand no chance against that she thought

Yvette held her breath. Had they seen her. Probably not because if they had there would be a hail of bullets by now. The unit rattled on towards the farm. She slowly got up and brushed down her muddy skirt. She felt helpless because she couldn't warn Pascal. It was then she felt a sticky liquid oozing from her satchel. The eggs were all broken.

Eight

NO COMPROMISE

The next day Le Rat came back to the farm. He was alone. After courtesies he said "Today we go and meet one of the main resistance leaders. His name is Andre, some-what arrogant and a staunch communist but commands over 500 men of the FTP. (Francs-Tireurs et Partisans) in the Correze. He is based in Tulle, not far away but he is in our sector today so we will meet him about an hour. Although a literary man with many novels to his credit, don't mistake him for a soft intellectual. He fought in the Spanish Civil war and is tough. He is desperate to have a strike at the Germans. Your job is to convince him that would be hopeless. Not only hopeless, suicide"

They set off on bikes along winding uphill roads that became, after an hour, almost an unsurfaced track. There was a shepherd's hut on the roadside surrounded by rocky terrain and a few sapling trees. This was Claude's first major activity and weeks of doing very little had started to work on his hamstrings until he felt them red hot.

They got off the bikes just as the door opened. A man of medium build with jet black hair cropped close to his skull and wearing black dungarees with a red neckerchief stood there, looked around, told them to put the bikes out of view around the back, then waved them in. It was dark inside.

There was nothing in the hut except an old table and chairs but gradually Claude could make out the two other men with rifles sat in the corner. Le Rat introduced them. "thank you for meeting us" he said. "This is Captain Claude Buckingham from SOE London. He is on a reconnaissance mission in the Montauban sector. I thought it would be good for you both to meet as Claude has a direct line to London"

Andre Malraux said nothing for a few minutes then produced a bottle of cognac and three glasses from under the table. He poured a generous slug to each of them and raised his glass in silence. Then he said in a quiet voice "Why is London sending us so few weapons. All they send us last month was one Sten gun, some pencil detonators, a few Welrod pistols (bolt action and very quiet when fired) and plastic explosives. How do the British intend us to fight the Bosch with that "bicycle pump" (This was the nickname given to the Welrod which resembled a tube when the butt and magazine were detached to make it less bulky and obvious to carry). We need many more Sten guns, rifles, grenades, ammunition and medical supplies. We have to steal old world war one guns from the Bosch" and with that he picked up standard infantry Mauser rifle propped against the table. "This is useless for ambush and close quarter fighting."

There was silence, then Claude spoke. "My orders from London are to tell you not to fight open pitched battles with the Germans. You will never win. You will be wiped out and so will all your families because the Germans will take reprisals for every soldier you kill. And certainly, do not capture and kill any high- ranking officer. The Germans around here are not front -line soldiers, they are only garrison troops supervising the policing of the area. If you want a fight, then it's the Vichy French who are doing more harm to you than the Germans. And by the way we can give you instructions on how to make Sten guns- very easy and cheap, maybe 5 francs each and you can use German 9 mm ammunition"

Andre was quiet for a moment then said. "How can you know what it is like to live under the Bosch invaders? Sleeping in our beds and eating all our food. Our daily lives are subject to deportations and killings. We can't get clothes and we are suffering from illnesses like tuberculosis. And we have never forgiven our leaders who stopped fighting when we had an army of over five million against their two million and the best and biggest tanks. We were betrayed. The Bosch ran around our Maginot line like foxes chasing sheep. It was humiliating We will settle all scores with the collaborators in due course, but our job is to rid France of the Bosch. In my previous life I admired one your greatest British adventurers T.E Lawrence, aka Lawrence of Arabia. He was a scholar, a soldier and wanted nothing more than to rid Arabia of Turks. I admired him; he was a man with the need for the "absolute", for whom no compromise was possible and for whom going all the way was the only way.

He should be remembered not just as a guerrilla leader in the Arab revolt and the British liaisons officer with Emir Faisal but also as a romantic lyrical writer. I have read all his works and they inspired me to be an adventurer and go to French Indo China before I came back and fought for the ideals of the Spanish civil war. We need to be like Lawrence – no compromise, drive the Bosch out by any means."

"You have a good knowledge of our history" said Claude 'but I must strongly advise against spoiling for a fight. We have had experience of that in 1942 when we encouraged British parachutists to commit the assassination of the murderous Reinhard Heydrich in Prague and then the terrible revenge taken by the Germans against the village of Lidice; it was completely erased, and hundreds of thousands died. We are not going to support you doing that. And here in France in last year our two circuits were broken and we must start again. We will support you with every means possible to sabotage key installations, railways, airfields, and ammunition dumps; but open battle – no. This is the only way ahead; I am showing you the forest of future hope but all you can see are yesterday's trees. Ask for what you want from London, le Rat will take the request but whatever you do please consider my advice and pass the message on."

Andre rose and said thank you for coming. The meeting was over. Nothing more was said, both had made their points of view well known; like Lawrence, there was no compromise.

Le Rat and Claude cycled back in silence. At the farm Le Rat said "I am sorry he was so obstinate but anything less he would have lost face with his followers. I will watch him for you and let you know if anything major happens. However, there is one advantage we have – he has nothing solid to fight against except old German soldiers who pose no threat so maybe all will be calm until the Allies land."

"Thanks for arranging the meeting and I will see what I can do to influence London to send more Sten guns at least or even the plans on how to make them – they are very simple mechanically," said Claude. Then Le Rat added "I have to tell you that I was told there are two RAF officers making their way down the "Comet" escape route from northern France to Spain so the Germans may be more alert and conducting more regular patrols. I don't know any more than that but be careful." Claude had been told about "The freedom trail" but had never met anyone involved. That was about to change.

Nine

THOROUGH SEARCH

Pascal heard a motor bike and clank of a half- tracked vehicle coming up the road. He ran inside the farmhouse and told his parents who were now eating at the table to stay calm. Then he went back outside and picked up the axe and continued chopping the wood. The motorcycle combo came into the yard followed by the halftrack. The Major got out of the side car and saluted. Pascal spoke in German, his native Alsace tongue: "good afternoon, Herr Mayor. What brings you and your men here?" The Major walked closer to Pascal. "Hello Pascal (Pascal was well known to the Germans on behalf of the chicken and pork he provided.) We are looking for two British Airmen who are hiding in the area. I would like my men to conduct a search of your house. I suppose you have nothing to tell me?" he said.

Pascal swallowed and relaxed a little. Tension and sweat ran away from his muscles like an open tap. If they were searching for arms and bombs that would be different but all these soldiers and firepower were just after two RAF pilots so Pascal could reply with all sincerity "Sorry Her Major, but there are no British airmen here, so please come and have some refreshment." The Major commanded his men to disembark the halftrack and told them to go search the barn, the house and everywhere around the perimeter. Pascal moved towards the house and the major followed. "Would you like glass of water or maybe something stronger" asked Pascal. "I would like both please" answered the German. Inside Paul introduced the major to his parents. They said nothing and just stared an icy stare born of distaste and hatred. Pascal poured a glass of fresh well water into a glass and then a small cognac into another glass. "Ah so, thank you very much Pascal, now we must search the house please." Before he gave the command to his troop, he downed the water and then the cognac. Nothing like this had ever happened before and Pascal could tell his parents were getting twitchy. He poured them each a cognac. The Major waited, slapping his gloves idly against his jodhpurs. "Have you seen or heard of any British airmen in the neighbourhood, please be careful when you answer. They tell me that you are a loyal citizen, in fact being from Alsace you are one of us and have never given any trouble, but it is my duty to tell you that hiding enemies of the state is a serious matter and you and your family risk deportation if we find British airmen here." His tone was sterner now. The Parents said nothing, and Pascal quietly replied that he had no knowledge whatsoever of such an event. The major summoned his men and told them to conduct a thorough search of the house and property. The search took over half an hour and Pascal was slightly shocked at the thoroughness of it all. He was slightly concerned that there was not enough hay on the barn floor hiding the trap door to the cellar below with its cache of arms and bombes but there was nothing he could do about that now.

Ten

SIBLING JEALOUSY

MONDAY MARCH 6, 1944, 90%FULL MOON WEATHER 13C FAIR

Yves and Yvette usually got on well for brother and sister, but Yves was suddenly very bubbly and happy He started helping more around the house and running errands for their mother. She noticed it with a smile but said nothing. "Yvette was straight to the point like a dagger to the heart "what's making you so happy?" asked Yvette.

Yves said nothing.

"Has my little brother got a girl friend?" Yves pointed his thumb against his nose at her "You're not the only one with a love life" he said and ducked the wooden spoon she threw at him.

"Do I know her?"

"No"

Is she older than me?"

"Not saying"

"Is she in my class at school?"

"Not telling"

With that Yvette punched her brother hard on the arm.

"Ouch, now you're going to die!"

But Yvette skipped around the kitchen and darted outside into the road.

Her mother restrained Yves from running after her.

Yvette walked into the square and the first person she met was Paul.

"Hello Paul, how are things at the garage."

"Everything's good but we now have so much more work with the German vehicles. They have been using them more than usual and need more maintenance than the Germans can cope with. Its only small things but as long as we can get the parts its good easy business"

"How is Raul and the railway yard?"

"No change but Raul does keep saying that Hans mutters about rumours from further up the line at Orleans"

"But that's a long way away from here; what sorts of rumours?"

"Increased troop movements"

"Paul, do you know if my little brother has a girlfriend?"

"Yes" he said, "and very pretty she is too." Yvette snorted.

"What's her name?"

"Aha, little miss inquisitive are we now".

"Come on Paul, or I won't bring you any eggs from Pascal" she said.

"Well, her name is Teresa, but everyone calls her Terri for short and she is something of a tom-boy anyway so the name fits. She is probably a year older than you and a tough kid. She lives on the outskirts of town and has three elder brothers and two younger ones, so she gets a lot of rough and tumble at home. She is always stealing things from the Germans, food mainly and I am told she is a crack shot with a rifle when she and her brothers go hunting for rabbits. And she is deft with a knife, she can skin a rabbit before you can say sacre-bleu!"

"Isn't that dangerous" Yvette said.

"Not really, they know where to go and the Germans don't stop them. In fact, the Old Guys here probably couldn't run fast enough to catch them."

Well fancy that thought Yvette; my little brothers' secret life; I wonder what she sees in him anyway.

Yvette thanked Paul and carried on down to the river pausing on the bridge to stare at the waters flowing endlessly from mountain to sea. It was so true what her teacher told her: 'you can't stand in the same water twice. Life is the same; you can't repeat the moment lost so live in it and live for the day'

She wandered on down to the train tracks; Raul and Hans were in the signal box as usual.

"Can I come up?" she said. The soldier on guard at the bottom motioned her to go up and she climbed up into the box with all its levers, buttons, bells, and maps.

"Hello Yvette why aren't you at school?" asked Raul. "The school is being repainted today. They got permission

49

to mix up some white lime stuff to coat the walls with. At least it will be nice and bright when we go back. Can I pull a lever?"

"You can try" said Raul knowing that it would be too hard for her. He was right. She puffed and gave up.

Hans looked on in amusement.

"Do You like trains" he said

Yes, I do, I love it when we can all go up to Tulle and see our Uncle, Father Antoine; he is the priest there for the commune and he is such a jolly fellow. It's always a nice day out especially in the summer with the lovely mountainous countryside around the Correze."

Then a bell rang in the box and Raul pulled two levers down and pushed one up.

"Here is the 1630 from Toulouse" said Raul. She then heard the whistle and saw the smoke coming round the bend ahead of the locomotive which ran up the slight gradient with ease into the station with only five coaches.

Yvette watched curiously at the mixture of passengers that got off; men with little suitcases,' ladies with baskets and some with crates of chickens from the markets and farms south of Toulouse, mothers with babies and of course soldiers in their field green Wehrmacht uniforms. Other soldiers waiting on the platform got on. The engine sounded a short whistle and pulled away working hard on the incline up to Cahors, the next stop.

"Where is the train going to?" asked Yvette.

"This one will terminate at Limoges" said Raul.

"Well thanks Raul, I had better be going to help mum with the supper.

She climbed down from the box conscious of the guard looking intently at her and went home.

"Hello Mum" she said when she entered the house "what's for supper tonight"

"Rabbit" said her mum.

Eleven

RABBIT GIRL

MARCH 16TH

All was quiet at the farmhouse of Madam Le Grange. Claude and Jenny went for walks in the woods and saw no one. The Germans were not venturing out of Montauban except with a full military escort. It was getting dangerous for an individual to go out alone with the trigger happy Maquis around. He had reported back the meeting with Le Rat and Robert Rossi. Buckmaster was not surprised. His coded reply to Claude was to follow instructions and hold the course and that he would be sending a special courier to the region shortly. Details to follow later.

There were minor reports of insurgences around Tulle and Brive, nothing serious. The Germans and especially the Gestapo were more intent on shipping their loot back to Germany now. Claude was amazed that they had the capacity to use trains for this purpose and also for the transports of Jews that kept rolling east. Why at this late stage in the war where they still doing this? Did the hatred of the Jews override even military traffic? They had unconfirmed reports that the Lyons area was experiencing more and more arrests of agents and that several small circuits had been broken. The Germans were using more sophisticated radio tracking systems and that coupled with arrests and torture provided them with the information needed for arrests. In fact, radio sets were becoming less numerous and the communications between Limoges and Lyons were getting scrappy. But where they were hiding, Claude and Jenny were relatively safe. There were no hot spots and there was little for Claude to report on in this quiet sector. He was finding it difficult to get the Maquis bands together; they were spread out in the hills. Madam Le Grange did her weekly visit to the market in Montauban to sell her eggs, bacon, and poultry; and to pick up any gossip from the inhabitants. The only thing of any interest was the continued rumours of allied airmen moving down from the north along the escape route known as 'The freedom Trail' or chemin de la liberté that passed right through Montauban and Toulouse to Saint Girons in the Ariege Pyrenees, then a six-day hike over a high Spanish mountain route carefully chosen to avoid all official checkpoints and German patrols and then to Barcelona in Spain. There were increased number of patrols to try and find them.

But this part of France was a nightmare for the Germans to patrol, short on troops, trying to cover vast areas of countryside, woods, rivers and mountains down into Spain. The French guides or'Passeurs' knew their business, Moving only 2 or three airman at a time and laying low during the day in safe houses. No one had approached them at the farm yet to help in their passage. Petrol had now become impossible to get so the farm renovated an old charcoal burner truck, the Gazogene invented by Citroen and of which at least 200 were used in the war, giving the car a top speed of 65 miles per hour for 30 mins. Trucks were converted and were slower but for trucks and cars to run on trees was an amazing invention. The Germans preferred horses to move their armies; only 10% of the German armed forces were mechanised, these being the armoured divisions and the Panzers. The Germans had stripped all the farms for miles around for horses. They seemed to have an affinity for horses, maybe Claude thought due to their agricultural upbringing in Germany. Both the French radio and the BBC had reports of increased atrocities by the Germans, more people shot by the French Milice who found that easier and quicker than employing the guillotine and the growing impatience of the French everywhere who kept asking about the allies "when will they ever come."

Yvette was very quiet when she sat down to supper. "How did you get the rabbit?' she asked although she could guess. "Ah," her mother said, "an anonymous friend of Yves gave it to him."

Yves smirked and said nothing. It was cooked in wine with onions and potatoes.

"I know where it came from" she said sourly "Yves has got a secret girlfriend but what she sees in this little runt I've no idea." That prompted a soggy piece of bread flying to Yvette's face.

"Stop it both of you. We are very grateful for whoever gave it to Yves. I don't want to know who owns the shotgun or the rifle used. No knowledge is safe knowledge." Said Francois.

"Her name is Teresa, Terri for short and she runs with a wild bunch from the outskirts of town "said Yvette. That prompted another even more soggy crust of bread flying at Yvette's face and leaving Rabbit sauce running down her face. Yvette got up to retaliate, but her mother was up first brandishing the rolling pin from the side table. "Anymore, and both of you go to bed without any supper" she barked. After that the rest of the meal was relatively civilised. But Yves had won the day and was a little hero in his mother' s eyes for being so resourceful.

Twelve

DAS REICH ARRIVES

THURSDAY APRIL 6, 1944, FULL MOON
96%, DRY AND 16 DEGREES

R aoul heard it first. It came in a flurry of French telegraphic orders for train traffic movements that night all the way from Poland into France. Whole trains were being requisitioned by the army, locomotives, carriages, box cars and significantly flatbed wagons. Raoul asked Hans asked if he had had heard anything from the German Deutsche Reich Bahn but the answer was "look the sentries are the last to know. Maybe your friends in the resistance may know something" said Hans, half hoping the Maquis could provide an answer, and half said in jest because he knew Raoul had decided a long time ago not to have anything to do with the resistance. It was more than a risk for him and his family, it probably meant death for him and a camp for his family.

The next people to have any real information was

Bletchley Park code breakers in England. They had intercepted German High command instructions from Adolph Hitler agreeing to the transfer of a whole SS division from eastern Poland down to Bordeaux in south west France. This news was communicated to Claude and Jenny in the farmhouse that night. They didn't mention it to madam Le Grange because they had no real instructions, these were to follow. Claude wondered why the Germans were stripping their eastern front at a time when the red army was pushing forward on all fronts. And which SS division was it? Claude knew from local gossip that the 3rd SS Totenkopf "Deaths Head" division had spent time down in Bordeaux area a few years ago, refitting and resting before their return to the cauldron of the Kursk battlefield in August 1943. Surely, they weren't coming back, because their reputation around Montauban had been one of pretty horrible 'Acktions' against the locals. They wouldn't be welcome. Maybe German high command was afraid of an allied landing around Bordeaux or on the coast of Southern France around Marseilles. But that seemed a presumptuous assumption to Claude "Maybe they have been so badly beaten up by the ruskies, that they need a rest and refitting,' said Jenny. 'Yes, maybe you're right Jenny, we will know soon enough," said Terri.

The next morning, they knew. It wasn't the 3rd SS Division Totenkopf; over the ether from Bletchley came the signal: "2nd SS Division '*Das Reich*' moving to Montauban for complete refitting and replenishment men and materials. Stop. Observe and report strength. End."

'So, this was it; SS *Das Reich*, SS Totenkopf and SS

1st Division 'Leibstandarte' were the three finest fighting divisions the Waffen SS possessed, probably the best fighting divisions of WW2; they were continuously fighting odds of ten to one; they were fanatical; they never yielded an inch in battle. Hitler had come to rely on them not only as his personal bodyguards but helping the regular Wehrmacht when they got into trouble and were surrounded by Russians which happened time and time again; Field Marshall Walter Model requested their help repeatedly to drive back the Russians when they surrounded the Wehrmacht units. They became known as 'Hitler's fire brigade". All three suffered horrendous losses, starved of fuel and supplies, fighting against ten to one odd, or more, and faced with overwhelming air power, their loyalty and fanaticism saw them achieve impossible victories. They recruited men starved of opportunity in the 1930's and Hitler built them up, gave them smart uniforms and pride. No other fighting divisions in any WW11 army came close to matching their performance.

So, On April 6, 1944, the 2nd SS armoured division *Das Reich* moved to the south-west of France, in a geography triangle ranging from Tonneins in Lot-et-Garonne to Caylus in Tarn-et-Garonne and Villefranche from Lauragais in Haute-Garonne. In Montauban, the staff of the *Das Reich* division and its commander Lanschültz, settled at the Calvin Institute located at 18 quai Montmurat (winter and spring 1944) before leaving Montauban on June 6, 1944, for the most part. High-ranking officers of the Wehrmacht and the SS stayed there regularly. On the other hand, torture rooms were quickly set up at the headquarters of the Gestapo, which had requisitioned a private mansion, the Hôtel de Vezin, located at 3 Faubourg du Moustier in Montauban. (This mansion was used during the filming of the film "Le vieux fusil" (The Old Rifle) with Philippe Noiret and Romy Schneider by Robert Enrico, you can also see some views of the Calvin Institute there when the German troops enter the city) The Kommandantur moved in on its arrival, back in April 1942, at the Hotel Terminus (23 avenue de Mayenne, opposite the Montauban SNCF station), then it took take up its quarters at the Hôtel du midi (12 rue Notre Dame, (current Mercure hotel) on the cathedral square). The German troops were installed in all the barracks of the city and the barracks of the current 17th RGP (Régiment du Génie Parachutiste) at the time Caserne des Dragons, located in front of the Cours Foucault, which also served as a prison, in particular for the 800 residents of the Lot arrested and rounded up in the Figeac region on May 12, 1944. The arsenal of Montauban was also requisitioned for the German troops and the *Das Reich* division to store materials, vehicles and ammunition there. (Information Courtesy of Montauban tourist office museum)

Claude debated what to do next. It would be several days before they arrived. Anyway, he told Madam Le Grange of the "rumour". She was shocked and very nervous.

"I hope my daughters and their families won' t be harmed;"

"Don't worry, the Germans will have other things on their minds, they will need the abattoir even more and as long as everyone behaves themselves then the Germans will do so as well."

Terri knew that she would spread the word in the town and alert the Maquis, but he knew that Le Rat would want him to meet up with Andre Malraux again. And Claude knew he would have to use all his powers of persuasion to deter the FTP having "a crack" at these so-called super soldiers.

The next day the news had spread throughout Montauban. Raoul asked Hans did he know about this "*Das Reich*" division. "Well, they were created from very lowly German stock and given a pride in themselves. They were catapulted over the ordinary army into an aura of prestige, given the best uniforms, equipment, training, and they acquired a sense of Knights Templar, being very chivalrous amongst themselves and very correct to the civilian population, paying their bills and not molesting the girls. If there was any bad conduct with women, the offending man or officer would be sent to a concentration camp like Dachau for a month; it never happened twice. However, I did hear stories that in Russia they regarded the population as untermensch, or subhuman so things got out of control there."

"Wow, that's a bit extreme," said Raoul. "I suppose they thought of themselves as better than other soldiers"

"Yes, Discipline was paramount, it worked. But they were merciless to their enemies. Although it was the civilian population that fared the worst, they respected a courageous enemy as an equal."

By now Yves, Yvette and Francoise had heard from Paul about the news. Madelaine said "well it will be good and bad; good because there will be more bread to bake, and more to sell but bad because I simply don't know where I will get the flour from"

Yvette was now desperate to see Pascal and to know that he was safe.

Thirteen

THERESA INTERVENES

It was already dusk when Yvette decided to go talk to Raoul down at the station yard, she felt she needed to get information about Pascal. She changed her normal jacket for something less informal. Raoul and Pascals parents were old friends and at least he might have heard any news. She wandered down the largely deserted streets to the marshalling yard and waved up at the signal box. Raoul looked at Hans who nodded an ok for her to come up. She always felt she was climbing into a special place, where these two men controlled the whole world; Raoul with his levers and signals controlled everything that moved in their little world and Hans represented the bigger world where everything was controlled by his German state.

'Hi Raoul, how are you and what have you been doing all day up here with Hans in your Eagles nest?' she liked to tease them and even Hans showed his human side by teasing back.

"what says the little schoolgirl to men of the world?'

he retorted. 'Shouldn't you be in bed now?' Raoul laughed and added 'Our little schoolgirl is pining for her boyfriend. She hasn't seen him for a few weeks' Yvette blushed and resented it when they made fun of her, but she stuck to her guns.

'Do you know where Pascal is? I thought you might have heard from his parents'

"No, I have heard nothing from the family since last week when they were all well but lying low because of the German patrols looking for escaped English airmen, and they don't want to be caught up in that' This was said as much to let Hans know that they were good citizens as it was to tell Yvette the truth. Just then a bell sounded in the box and Raoul pulled two levers saying 'Here comes the last train, its early tonight which is good because it means there's been no sabotage. When the Maquis pull out four sleeper bolts from the tracks, it causes so much disruption and for what? The Germans have a wagon of railway men on every train and the damage is soon repaired. It's not worth it"Ach, you are so right,' said Hans. 'And it makes us late getting back to our beds too. It's a nuisance'

They could hear the train running through the ravine outside the town, then rumbling across the town bridge, with a short sharp pull on the whistle to acknowledge the last signal in her favour and with embers falling from the funnel into the river as the driver shut down the fire with plenty of steam left in the boiler to travel into the platform.

Raoul threw all the signals to dead stop as he had done countless times before and turned to Yvette.

"That's it for another day, run along now before you

get int trouble, its late already and you will risk breaking the curfew'

Yvette turned and thanked them both, then half climbed, half jumped down from the signal box and hurried her pace out of the yard towards the station exit.

Just then came the order to halt; there was a new extra German guard on patrol with a big Alsatian dog in tow. Yvette stopped dead.

"Your papers please.' He said, Yvette fumbled in her coat but then her heart skipped a beat. She had left her papers in her other coat. How stupid she mumbled. She apologised to the guard for her stupidity. But he was not one of the normal older soldiers who you could pout and smile at; this was a much younger man.

'Name, address, and why are you here?' he asked. The dog, sensing a change in tone from his master, growled menacingly. Yvette was scared. She gave her details, and they were noted down adding that she had been to visit friends.

'Who are these friends please?' he asked.

Yvette knew enough to know that visiting the signal box was irregular and she couldn't tell him that. She hesitated. Just then another girl came up who had overheard the conversation and said "she came to visit me about some schoolwork'

The guard now unslung his rifle and half pointed it at the newcomer who had surprised him. The dog barked and strained at his chain.

'Papers please' he demanded. The girl handed them over saying that Yvette and she were good friends in the same class at school and that she would take care of Yvette and take her home. She was a very pretty girl and had an air about her, almost a swagger of defiance. Her eyes were dark brown and blazed with intensity, mirroring the depth of conviction and strength within her. She was not dressed in school uniform as was Yvette; she wore jeans and a Buisson Noir jacket, giving her an age of five years older than she really was.

'So, what is your full name?'

'My name is Theresa Pastor, but "with the biggest pouted lips and smile Yvette had ever seen added 'you can call me Terri'. This bravado had the desired effect.

The guard shouldered his rifle, satisfied that these two schoolgirls were not Maquis and told them both to scarper shouting "allez, allez". They both ran to the main road.

Yvette stopped and said 'Thank you so much for your help, I was in trouble there. Why did you help me? Do I know you? If you are really in the same school how come I've never seen, you?' 'Well, I am a year above you and to be honest I haven't been at school for over a year now, waste of time. But I helped you because I know your little brother Yves, he's cute'

You are the rabbit girl thought Yvette. They walked to the bridge together then Theresa turned west, and Yvette crossed the river with the waters ruffled into little breaking wavelets as the southwest wind from the ocean piled up the surface.

Fourteen

BIRTHDAY

The next day was Yvette's birthday. The bakery made her a cake, and someone found a big candle. Yvette was now 20 years old and the old "teenager" jokes were behind her. She felt happy and hoped that she would see Pascal today; maybe he would give her a little present. Perhaps a chicken or maybe he would have shot a rabbit for her. All the family sat round including Madelaine from the bakery. Francois had managed to find a little sugar and liberally sprinkled it on top of the cake. Madam Francois opened a bottle of champagne, and everyone had a glass. They sang Bon Anniversaire- happy birthday twice because Yves her brother liked the song.

Then Francois produced a little packet and with a kiss on her head gave it to Yvette, who was so excited. She tore open the old paper it was wrapped in and out fell a lovely, perfumed bar of white creamy soap tinged with blue. This was totally unlike the square bricks of hard Marseille soap. It smelt of lavender. She put it to her cheek and felt the smoothness. 'Thank you, dear mama. I have never had my own soap before, and this is a lovely little treasure." In war time one used up gifts hidden before the war; there was nothing in the shops anyway, so they made do with resources at hand, mostly sand and hot water for washing. She had really dreamed of new shoes; her old leather ones were tattered to shreds, and she hated the wooden clogs everyone had been issued with because the Germans had confiscated all the leather for the Wehrmacht. Anyway, Yvette was very happy with the lovely, scented soap. Her mother said, "the scent is from the lavender grown in Provence. We only had a drop of the oil left; that's why it's such a pale colour, it's good for your skin and for your spirit." They finished the champagne.

Fifteen

ROUND UP

They came for Pascal early the next morning, April 7th. He was outside in the barnyard. The black Citroen pulled up in front of him and three men got out, a Gendarme, one who looked like a builder and a man in a trench coat with a brief case and black hat. "Good morning, what can I do for you?' said Pascal. The man with the hat spoke first. "Do you know who I am? "he said. Pascal said no. "I am Oberfurher Trascal, the new gestapo officer here. We would like to speak with you in private.' Pascal led the way into the kitchen. He recognised the Gendarme; his name was Pierre and he and Pascal had started at school together. Pascal said nothing. He made four cups of coffee while the German sat down and opened his brief case and spread some papers and files across the table.

So, he so he said this is Pierre, but you already know him and this is Jerome my driver; tell me about your farm here." Well, we have a small farm, we don't have many animals anymore because they've all been requisitioned stolen or eaten. I live here with my parents, we moved here about 20 years ago, from Alsace, so I speak German and French and maybe a little Dutch. I look after the few horses we have, and I sell some eggs. it is very quiet here and we don't see many Germans or even French people for that matter

'So' Trascal said, you don't have any dealings with the Maquis, you're not hiding any arms or enemies of the state or any escaped prisoners of war, in fact Pierre tells me you're a model citizen which is a bit suspicious in itself; there's always something lurking under everybody's exterior but that doesn't matter. I know our Wehrmacht friends have had a good look round and they found nothing, that is to your credit but now we have a different opportunity for you, our glorious Fatherland is in need of more soldiers and we decided that you should join one of the elite German divisions currently being put together back in Alsace to fight the Russians or to fight the Americans when they come because they will come, they will surely come. Pascal sat bolt upright and said 'I'm not going back to Alsace as I have a farm here, I have to maintain it and besides this is a German war not anything to do with Alsace. This would be an outrage, forced conscription.

'That's where you're wrong, this is everybody's war and the French are rising up against us although we have done nothing to them, we've paid all our restaurant bills, we are taking nothing for granted, we behaved as proper German soldiers to your women but there are other forces at work here, there is a growing element of antagonism against us in France but that's beside the point we need strong young men like you of German if not German /French origin to come and fight for the Fatherland. There are many young men from Alsace already who are fighting in our army particularly against Russia, maybe some 200,000 so you are not alone, you're not unique and you will have joined up with old comrades from your old area. In fact, you will join an elite Waffen SS division specially created for Alsace volunteers"

Pascal said nothing, his mind working furiously, it would mean that he may never see his farm again, in fact he might not even see his parents again because he had heard stories about the Russian front and its brutality.

Pascal said, "well if it's alright with you Herr Trascal, I would rather not volunteer for this opportunity"

The German shifted in his chair then with a smile which is more of a grimace, he said,

"I am afraid you have no option; I have been empowered to round up likely young man to come and join our side and you will leave today. In the meantime, I'll post a guard here so you with orders to shoot you if you do try to escape. We have enough evidence against you to ship you to a camp straight away, black marketeeing, hiding arms, helping Jewish prisoners escape, attending illegal parachute drops – someone with a grudge has told us about you. For all of this I could have you shot now; but you have a choice. I am being generous. And even if you do escape, your parents will be shipped to a camp, they may not even survive the journey let alone the camp, your farm burnt and everything destroyed, including the animals."

Pascal look aghast at Pierre and Pierre shifted uneasily;

his eyes went down to the floor. Pascal said "Pierre, you can't be part of this? We have known each other for years, since first school.

Pierre then said "I'm very afraid Pascal that all this is correct and I have to go along with it, my wife is suffering from pneumonia and the only medicine I can get for her is from the Germans and Herr Trascal has been very helpful in procuring these medicines for me so I am powerless to do anything, they have got me under their control and as much as I love France and I love you, I can't do anything but to all help organise your departure and look after things when you are gone.'

With that the gestapo officer pulled out a gun from his pocket and laid it on the table. Pierre did the same this was going to be a forced journey and who knows what awaited him in Alsace. "Well, I have to say goodbye to my parents," said Pascal 'they are still asleep upstairs, but I can go wake them or they will be down here in a minute if you care to wait"

"We have all the time in the world" said the gestapo officer but you must be on the road by mid-day and join the train tonight at Poitier.

When Pascal told his parents later that morning they were horrified. "listen, that's exactly why we got away from Alsace' said his father. "the age-old Cauldron of bubbling enmity between French and Germans. Just because you're blonde with blue eyes that doesn't make you a true blood Arian, you are born an Alsatian and you have every right to a separate identity. And as for being betrayed, maybe you have by some vindictive jealous neighbour, maybe its madam Didier at the next farm because she thinks you've got a gun. We don't need to sacrifice our son" Everybody listened in silence.

"I'm sorry" I said the gestapo officer "but everybody is making sacrifices and you will have to make the same sacrifices as other. He is going to join a good cause, for the fatherland and the protection of Alsace from the barbaric Russian hordes"

"A good cause" said the father "that is ridiculous, this is not a good cause that you're fighting this German war for against France and against everybody else, it's an insane war I am not going to let you take my son"

Trusler sighed, "I'm sorry but you have no choice, now let Pascal get his things together and then we can do this in a gentlemanly way; normally I would come here with a whole squad of Wehrmacht soldiers and Pascal would have been bundled into a truck and taken away but because Pierre has spoken highly of you, I thought we would play this a little bit more gentlemanly. Don't try my patience, please hurry up Pascal, get everything in order and we will leave. We will go from here down to Montauban and then from there we will drive you up to Poitier where you will join a train for Alsace tonight"

Pascal looked at his parents and said, "It's all right, "Herr Trusler has explained what will happen if I resist and Pierre has promised to help when I'm gone. After all, the war can't go on much longer. The Allies will arrive soon, and the Russians are already entering Kiev."

Pascal got a few warm clothes together. Then they left and went to the police station in Montauban where Pascal was issued with identity papers, passes, and ration cards. Soon after mi-day and a frugal meal of soup, bread and cheese, brought in by a German orderly, he was handcuffed to another gendarme and led to a big black Citroen, flying a gestapo flag from the bumper. The driver was German. Pascal had not even thought about Yvette; there wasn't time, he was sure Pierre would tell her. Then they set off on the six- hour drive to Poitier rail head, some 360 kilometers away.

Sixteen

BED BUGS

APRIL 8TH

Jenny woke early; she had had a bad night; she couldn't get comfortable on the straw paillasse and the straw pillow made her hair itch. She was sure she could feel lice scurrying around her scalp. But apart from hot water and soap she had nothing to get rid of them with. She tuned into her radio frequency; nothing. She was grateful that Claude had installed six 12-volt car batteries for the radio as it was dangerous to rely on the mains electric. The batteries were then charged up with a battery charger overnight every three days. Plenty of juice – the powerful set needed it. Claude was already at the kitchen table. And Madam was at the stove cooking eggs. A delicious smell of coffee came from the fire, which was always burning day and night with logs from the forest.

"well,' Claude said, 'you look all beat up this morning; bad night?" Jenny started scratching her head and madam said "ah, it's the Poux, the lice, they have been busy. Get some hot water, put salt into it and wash your hair. Then put olive oil on your head, rub it in well to suffocate those smaller ones that remain" Claude knew he had to meet up with Le Rat and find out from London what their instructions were. But he knew that he had to go and view things for himself in Montauban.

Madam Le Grange was working chopping up what looked like meat from a deer carcass. He said 'Madam, if I wanted to find out what's happening in the town, who is the best person to speak to?'

'You should speak to Raul in the signal box at the station; he knows all about train movements in France and if the Germans are planning anything special for this area, he will know. But be careful, the signal box will be guarded. If you can't speak to him, go to Café Flaubert by the bridge and speak to the owner, Rudi. He is a friend of mine and tell him I sent you. Take Jenny with you, make it look like you are lovers and go in and order a coffee and a cognac each to make it look like you are local French people.' Claude was hesitant about taking Jenny, partly in case she missed any transmissions and partly because he didn't want to expose her to unnecessary danger, but he could see the logic; a single man would be an obvious target. He thought about it then said, 'Good idea, come on Jenny, get dressed for town' Jenny snorted 'but I have a bad headache and these lice are killing me' "we will fix the headache and you can fix the lice when we return. Make sure you have your papers and identity cards with you' he said.

Claude put on his smart coloured bow tie and hat. Jenny said 'you look smart why the bow tie? 'ah well said

Claude every wine salesman has to have a bow tie, that is his signature he has to look as though he is the master of vines, it is very traditional, it is my signature" Jenny laughed.

They set off walking briskly for the town by the back way through the woods. Soon they arrived at the outskirts and Terri headed for the station. "why are we going to the station,' said Jenny. 'We need to buy tickets for Bordeaux in case we are stopped, then we can show that we are planning to return to the business. After all, I am supposed to be a wine merchant from there and you are my assistant, right?'

The town had an air of expectancy about it. One couldn't touch it, or smell it, but one could definitely feel it

At the station they bought they bought 2 return tickets to Bordeaux for that evening They headed for the cafe and sat at the table in the centre of the room, they bought 2 large coffees and slowly drank them as they watched out of the window at the large amount of troop activity. Then the patron came to the table with a newspaper and said maybe you would like to read this. Claude thanked him and opened the roll up rolled up newspaper – there was a scribbled note inside saying attention be careful of the two men sitting in the window. Claude looked at the two men who are dressed in mackintoshes and had hats on. He didn't like the look of what he saw, he knew immediately that they were Gestapo.

Claude and Jenny Quietly finished their coffee which had tasted terrible and then calmly got up and walked outside out in the street they looked around but suddenly the two Gestapo men were alongside them "papers please "they shouted. they both produced their papers and the biggest of the two men scrutinise them very carefully so why are you here they asked well I am a wine salesman from Bordeaux and I'm visiting clients here. "ach no, the big man said, I'm sure that there's not very many clients here for your very fine Bordeaux wines here". 'you would be surprised' said Claude the hotel Daville buy some of my excellent wines and then there are small places which buy small parcels of excellent quality wines to set aside their regular Cahors or Bergerac's."

"How long are you staying?' "we have a train ticket for tonight to return to Bordeaux said Claude "let me see it" Claude produced the train tickets "okay" said the fat man "but leave tonight and do not come back here ".

Claude and Jenny turned away with a sigh of relief, but they knew they had to stay till later because there had been a proclamation issued from a van and loudspeaker going up and down the street for all the citizens to gather in the main square at 5:00 PM and Claude knew that he had to attend that meeting.

Seventeen

PARADISE FOR DAS REICH

They went for a walk up to the River bridge, by now the town was full of vehicles, large lorries with troops in them and one lorry stacked as full as it could be with loaves of bread. The soldiers in the vehicles were very young and they looked up at amazement at the blue shuttered houses as they rolled through, they had never seen anything like this. Most of them had come from war torn and destructed areas of northern France Poland and Russia where there was hardly any pretty villages left but here in Montauban it looked as though they were in a different paradise; there is no war damage whatsoever and everything seemed normal for them and they couldn't help but look at the French girls parading in the streets and the French girls smiled back after all it had been a long time for some of these women without the menfolk who are now prisoners of war in Germany or who had left to join the maquisards in the hills, there was a joint feeling between them that the war had its place but love of life also had its place. Then they heard the whistle of a train in the distance they walked to the town bridge and soon the exhaust note of a heavily laden train was to be heard. People were now crowding around the bridge and then round the corner up across the bridge came two big powerful steam engines pulling at least 60 flat cars behind them, on the flatcars were tanks, they looked to Claude like mark 5 Panthers, there certainly weren't any Tiger tanks amongst them, the train slowly rolled on and was soon directed down into the sidings in Montauban.

By now it was just after 2:00 o'clock so they still had a long time to kill they walked through the town again and stopped at a different cafe slightly away from the main centre, here they asked for cognac and a glass of water. Jenny said I'm hungry "can't we get something to eat? so Claude asked for some bread, and they bought a baguette between the two of them which they hastily devoured. Jenny was aghast at the lack of food in the shops; everyone looked thin; it was no surprise, her own ration card allowed 10oz of bread a day, 2oz of cheese a week and there was no ration for pasta or chocolate. Also, alcohol was forbidden on Sundays which was a big blow for the French. She understood from Madam le Grange that women were forbidden to buy cigarettes.

Back at the signal box Raoul was busy pulling levers. the marshalling yard was large, but not big enough to take the train into one siding alone so the engines were detached and the first engine run back through the loop to the back of the train. 20 flat beds at a time were disconnected and pushed into three sidings. "wow" said Raoul, "this is a big amount of German Armour. I wonder what they're going to do with it." Hans said "it can't be just to deal with the maquisards. This is going to be a full division of men and materials coming in". Hans was right by late afternoon over 15,000 men had crammed into Montauban and were directed by the military police to the lagers.

Eighteen

WE ARE YOUR FRIENDS

At 1630 hours Claude and Jenny walked slowly to the town square there were already a lot of people there, but the square was surrounded by a ring of German soldiers.

There was a platform in the middle and at 1700 hours precisely general Lammerding approached with his orderly and a big black Alsatian dog; all three mounted the platform and the Alsatian dog sat obediently at the heal of the general

'Good afternoon' said General Lammerding, 'we are here as your friends, we are here to protect you and to make sure that all the daily activities of Montauban will continue, we shall not harm you and any of our troops that misbehave will be severely punished but in return you have behave and not harm our soldiers or our equipment. anybody caught sabotaging our tanks or vehicles will be shot. if any German soldier is shot then 10 people will be taken as hostages and shot in return, their houses burnt, and their family deported. There will be a new curfew starting at 20.00 hrs tonight. Any flags other than German ones will be burnt along with the house of the owner'. (little did they know but Claude had been told the French were hiding American and English flags up the drain-pipes). 'Anybody out after curfew will be regarded as hostile and an enemy of the Reich. Also, we will be confiscating bicycles because the maquisards get you people to act as bicycle reconnaissance units and there will be people here in this square who are helping them, already further up the line in Tulle and Brive there have been reports of guerrilla activity and German soldiers being killed, reprisals are taking place. Even the Geneva convention allows for retribution against franc-tireurs and bandits. But the *Das Reich* division is not here to chase bandits; your own gendarmes and Milice will do that. We are here to rest after an exhausting campaign in Russia and to re-equip in case there is an allied landing here in the Southwest, so you should know that we are not here to harm you and that everything will be alright as long as you behave'

Then Lammerding turned, the Alsatian dog immediately sensed the movement and rose very obediently, the general clicked heels, saluted "Heil Hitler", and dog and master both went out of the square, the adjutant following.

Nineteen

PIANO LESSONS

Claude and Jenny left and returned to the farmhouse. Jenny filed a report for London emphasising the miles of troops moving into the town. Where have they all come from, she thought. Surely there cannot be any men left in Germany considering the losses of the last few years. "Well said Claude, the Germans recruit and press men into service from the countries they have invaded, especially Rumanians, Hungarians, Danes, Norwegians, in fact anyone with ethnic German population. They copied the Romans."

Everybody had officers billeted on them and Yvette and family had an officer called Wolfgang. They gave him Yvette's room and she doubled up with her mother.

On the other side of town, Yvette was practicing the piano but when Wolfgang came in, he sat beside her and said, "I am now going to teach you a beautiful piece again by Bach called "sheep may safely graze". It's a simple tune composed by Bach. He wrote it for the birthday of a count, Duke Christian of Sachsen-Weissenfels, a man of big ambition and, by all accounts, an ego to match. He was a passionate huntsman, and Bach and his librettist Salomo Franck wrote the Hunting Cantata probably to mark his birthday on 23 February 1713. It's in B flat major. Wolfgang played it and then invited Yvette's to play. "That was very good" he said "you were note perfect but perfection in the notes may be one thing, it's how you play it is important. Your fingers should glide over the keys very lightly. Now some even easier pieces you can play are from Beethoven's sonatas like No8 in D major, they should be easy for you, and it will remind you of a lake with the waters lapping the shore. Let me play it for you'. It was a poignant piece and Yvette loved it, even more than Bach

It is true that Yvette had an immediate crush on Wolfgang. His handsome stature, smart uniform, his kindness to her and the household, his music, yes above all his music. It made her feel that if an orchestra composed of different nationalities could play together in harmony, why couldn't nations and politicians do the same. She asked Wolfgang. "Well politicians don't trust each other; musicians trust the music. It's their life. Yvette's then asked Wolfgang if he knew what had happened to Pascal; he had been picked up by the Gendarmes and nobody knew where he was. Could Wolfgang find out. Wolfgang was surprised as he knew nothing of this Pascal boy, but he said he would find out.

It was Yves who found out from Terri, rabbit girl, that Pascal had been taken away by the gestapo in a car and then to a railhead near Poitier – her contacts in the maquisards knew every movement there was concerning the Germans. Yves told his mum who advised him not to say anything to Yvette. Francoise knew that this would result in a terrible outburst and there was no knowing what Yvette would do if she knew.

Twenty

SPITFIRE ATTACK

F ive hours later just outside Poitiers, the driver apologised for the slow journey caused by the continuous checkpoints. The gendarme still handcuffed to Pascal was getting irritated. Everyone in the car was tired. The German soldier said nothing, so Pascal said nothing in return. The conversation en-route amounted to nothing more than pleasantries so Pascal slept as best he could. His limbs were very stiff They had only stopped once for fuel and to use the stinking hole in the café that passed for a toilet. At least the roads were now good and straight, and they were making up time.

The first they knew about the rogue Spitfire was when it had banked, right in front of them and came roaring down the long straight road outside Tours. It opened fire with its eight machine guns 100 metres away, just a short burst, maybe the last of the day, but it was enough to chew up the dirt and smack into the front of the car. The driver subconsciously threw the car left into the trees as abruptly as he could. It was too late; the fusillade strafed the engine and killed the German soldier in the front seat outright; the driver slumped over the wheel and the car hit the ditch and turned over, the engine smoking and then flaming. The Gendarme on Pascals left tried to avoid the tree that came screeching and crashing in through the side and dealing him a deathly head blow. Pascal, shielded by the Gendarme and the dead bodies in the front was dazed but unhurt. The car was lying on its side. His door was buckled, and the lock jammed. But first he had to get out of the handcuffs. He reached into the Gendarmes pocket, but the key wasn't there; maybe the other pocket but the tree trunk had wedged the man in and Pascal couldn't lift him up. The car was burning from the front to the back. The heat was becoming unbearable. Then he smelt the petrol and knew he had only seconds left before the car exploded. He tore at the Gendarmes jacket and felt inside. He could feel the key inside the pocket lining. Desperately he tore at the tough serge materiel. It wouldn't yield. The Gendarmes gun holster was lying on his right side within easy reach. Pascal unlatched it with his right hand, tore out the gun, cocked it and fired into the pocket. The hole created by the blast was enough to enable a tear to be made and the key came out, luckily undamaged by the bullet that buried itself into the bank underneath. He put a second shot into the car lock and lying back on top of the Gendarme used the power of both his legs to push against the door and the tree trunk. It sprang open and fell back. Pascal was now lying on his back and had to turn over and push himself with his arms to get his legs out first, toppling over and hitting his head against the roof as he catapulted out, feet first. He felt the blood flowing from his head but rolled over on the road just as the first explosion came. He kept on rolling as fast as he could across the road until he hit the opposite ditch. Then the car convulsed and was lifted several feet off the ground when the main explosion came, throwing car parts everywhere. Pascal hugged the bottom of the ditch. He lay there for several minutes thinking what to do. He was then conscious of someone standing in the field looking down on him. He turned and saw the farmer with his pitchfork about to spear him, thinking he was a German. Pascal yelled out in French for him to stop. The farmer hesitated but he heard Pascal say he was an escaped French prisoner and then he was pulled up to his feet and a large kerchief tied around his head. 'Ah mon pauvre, Come, let's go to the farmhouse as fast as we can' said the farmer,' who knew that a German patrol would be along very soon. But Pascal knew he was safe, damaged, hurt, but safe for the moment.

The farmhouse was just like the ones at home, except there were other people there. At least six men and one woman. The warmth of the fire made Pascal feel exhausted. Someone thrusted a cup of hot coffee into one hand and a glass of brandy into the other while another looked at his head wound. Désolé he said, 'we have nothing to give you for that but I will clean it and tie a bandage round it. The man peed into a cup and used the hot urine to sterilise the wound; and then washed that with clean cold water, tying a tight bandage around his head. Nobody said anything.

The farmer had told the group what he had seen at the car crash. Then the woman spoke.

'We have to be sure that this was a real accident and not staged by the Gestapo to penetrate our organisation. It just happens we were here picking up food and supplies so tell us who you are and where are you from' Pascal spoke slowly, he was still in a state of shock from having narrowly escaped death. He told them of his farm in Montauban, arrested to fight for Germans because he was from Alsace and was being transported east to join a unit. The woman introduced herself. 'I am known as Sylvie-because I slink in and out of the woods. These men are maquisards – Hugo with the beard, Gaspard, young Victor, Theo, old Jean, and Lucien. You will come with us and if you perform your first test well then, we will believe your story. If not, we will shoot you. In the meantime, I will check out your story with our friends down the line in Montauban.

They left the farm and walked across rutted fields to woods set on uplands. The path climbed steeply and brought them to another farmhouse. Pascal had to have help from big Hugo supporting his arm. Inside were five other men, farmers at first glance but clearly very well armed farmers with bandoliers and holster side arms. Sylvie introduced Pascal and related the background. One of the newcomers, a gruff bearded man said 'how do we know that he's not a German stooge in a fake accident? We cannot trust anyone, not since the Valerie betrayal. What's your full name and were you born?"

My name is Pascal Frédéric, and I am French from Alsace' answered pascal

'Or is your name Pascal Fredrich and you are German from Alsace,' said the gruff man.

I have French nationality, and a French mother and father; I do speak both French and German, but everybody in Alsace is bilingual; that's our fate of history' replied Pascal

Sylvie interrupted and then explained that Valerie a farmers' daughter infiltrated their organisation a year ago when there were 50 or more operatives; she meant well but she was desperately in love; she was a local girl married to a Frenchman who was sent away to Germany to work; she was distraught, and the foolish girl tried to buy him back and in return for a deal with the Gestapo she negotiated his freedom. The deal was informing on the circuit. Thirty operatives were caught and shipped off to Dachau. But worse was to happen. The Gestapo linked our circuit with the mother circuit in Lyons and there the Gestapo chief Klaus Barbie took a personal interest in that network, arresting two sisters and torturing one to death in front of the other by skinning her alive. The surviving sister didn't talk but was shot anyway"

"What happened' asked Pascal who was visibly shocked. "we dealt with Valerie like any other traitor. She was shot. And her husband died in the camp anyway. A pyrrhic victory." The rump of the rest of the circuit are here; we slipped away to live in the woods and gradually regrouped. We knew that the allies must come soon this year, so the risk was worth taking." Sylvie then said to the group 'The accident Pascal was in is genuine; he almost died; and his story is good. But he knows we will check it out in Montauban. And tomorrow he will come on our mission with us and prove himself. And we can use a good strong young man.' No one said anything else. They rested overnight and ate pork, bread, and root vegetables with a rough wine for supper. Sylvie then marshalled everyone together for the briefing. "Tomorrow we go and de-rail a troop train, our information is that one will pass down the line from Chateauroux to Limoges and we will hit it at the steep and very curved section just 5 kilometers from here. It will be going slowly up the twisty incline. We just have to de-rail it; we are not going to be so silly as to attack it. "But" said one, the Germans carry gangers on every train with rail sections and they can repair the track in an hour. Is it worth the risk? 'We will carefully camouflage the explosives; we want the engine to run off the rails into the track bed; they will need a crane to lift it back on. It could take a day and will block the line. No harm to come to the Germans otherwise there will be reprisals.'

Pascal now knew roughly where he was; he had escaped south of Poitiers and was now somewhere near Montmorillon or Bellac, probably the former if they were only 5 kilometers away from the main line. He had lost his bearings and wasn't aware that he had travelled or been taken so far East, nearly 30 kilometers deep into the countryside in Haute Vienne.

Twenty-One

SYLVIE'S PRACTICAL ADVICE

The next morning it was light before 0500 and they set off soon after that. Pascal was tasked with carrying the Bren gun, an English semi -automatic machine gun. Very accurate as a single shot over 1 kilometer and good for a burst of 500 rounds a minute. The limitation was the magazine; so, he also carried 10 clips of .303 standard army ammunition. "We are not going to get into a fire fight with the Germans and in any case if you use the Bren too long the barrel will overheat said Sylvie. Then you will have to piss on it to cool it down–that's not a girls' job!" Said Sylvie. She carried everything on her little frame; the plastic explosives and detonators; two stick grenades in her belt; and a Sten gun slung over her shoulders. Also boot polish for blackening the wires. It took them 2 hours to reach their destination. The going had been slow, moving through woods, up and down ravines, open ground and back to the woods. They now had a perfect view of the railway track as it wound like a wounded snake, around the hillside. It was still, very quiet and Pascal found it difficult to believe they hadn't seen or met anyone on their march, let alone Germans. 'Now' said Sylvie, 'Bruno here is my most trusted saboteur, trained in explosives; he has done this many times before, so listen and watch.' They unpacked everything including some odd-looking wedges of black wood. Pascal picked one up; it was very light and suddenly crumpled away in his hand. 'Those are more delicate and precious than the detonators' said Bruno 'I will show you. First we lay the charges; at both sides of the rail and at the next rail as well, all four charges linked together.' Bruno took the plastic explosive charges out and needed them like putty until they were soft; then he moulded them against the joint in the rails; 'you can do the next one he said'. Pascal followed his example. All this time Sylvie and the other 5 men were on guard. She had placed one on top of the hill and one just round the bends in both directions. She sat idly cleaning her Sten gun, calm and relaxed as though nothing on this bright summer's morning was troubling her in the world. Pascal more than glanced at her as he realised for the first time how attractive she was with her hair swept back in a ponytail, a cigarette in her lips blowing ringlets of smoke into the fresh air, and her lithe sculptured body at ease in her fatigues battle dress. Soon Bruno and Pascal had finished laying the charges, Bruno now ran the wires along the inside of the rails, using the boot polish to blacken the connecting wires, then gently pushing the stone ballast over everything to cover up any trace. 'The train will have a troop wagon being pushed in front of it with soldiers and trained railway observers in it looking for any irregularities on the track;

they will have eagle eyes so we must be super eagles to hide everything. 'Why have we laid four charges' asked Pascal, 'wont two do to break the track' Bruno smiled; "if we break the track, they can repair it; they would pull the lead wagon off the track and the engine will be undamaged. We have to get both lead wagon and engine onto our section between our two sections. The wires have been connected so that when the lead wagon hits the second rail connectors, all will explode together and now we have to knock the rail ties out and replace them with our little wedges we have brought with us. They will disintegrate as soon as a heavy locomotive passes over them; and with the explosions the rails will simply splinter sideways; the engine will then plough into the stone ballast. They can't repair that without a crane which will take hours to get.'

Pretty ingenious thought Pascal. 'Now finally we have to put detonators into our putty; I will do that as they need careful handling.' Bruno gingerly took each detonator, inserted it deeply into the Semtex, wired it and pushed the ballast stones over it. They stood back and Bruno motioned for Sylvie to come and inspect. She cast her eagle eye over the work which had taken the best part of an hour but as Pascal appreciated, it had to be done carefully and properly. 'Its good Bruno; let's go eat. She called the other three maquisards over and they retreated to a grassy knoll about fifty metres away. Sylvie opened the rucksack and took out bread and cooked chicken legs. Wow thought Pascal, she is a fighter and a mother to these guys. They all drank from their own water bottles. It was now 10:00 hrs and the warmth of the sun made Pascal feel drowsy. They maintained silence. They must not be heard or observed now, not even by a farmer or shepherd; no one could be trusted. Pascal whispered, 'what time is the train due?' Sylvie looked at her watch 'About thirty minutes' she whispered back. Fifteen minutes later she directed everyone to take up their positions in the trees. 'As soon as the job is done, we must escape at once back the way we came but we will split up, two one way two another way and Pascal you will come with me. Remember, no one is to shoot unless attacked.'

Twenty-Two

YOU ALWAYS REMEMBER THE FIRST

Bruno was the first to hear the sound of a train down in the valley, labouring up the incline. Then they all heard it, the rasping of the exhaust and sound of steam filling the air. They could see pillars of steam rising above the trees, still a way away. The sound of the wheels screeching on the curves as the flanges fought the rails and the pounding of the engine, clearly pulling a heavy load. Then it came into view around the bend; the engine was belching smoke and steam like a dragon; in front was the wagon packed with soldiers ready to jump out and attack any saboteurs that might be foolhardy to try any confrontation. Pascal could see the long line of coaches and flat beds with military equipment on snaking back down the incline. He fingered the Bren gun nervously. All he had been shown was the safety cock, how to load the magazines and how to clear a simple jam. Other than that, he did not know how it would perform for him. Sylvie had spaced the group out, all lying flat on the ground in a semi- circle with the Bren at one end. They waited with bated breath; would the charges be spotted. The answer came with the crump of the explosion and Pascal watched in amazement as the lead wagon and the locomotive splayed the rails apart and dug into the ballast with a sickening scraping and banging. Unfortunately, the lead wagon was pushed up into the air as it dug into the sleepers and the unstoppable power of the engine ploughed forward. Men tumbled out, some landing badly. Then the air was rent with commands being barked and a machine gun situated on top of the first coach barked into action, sweeping left and right. 'Time to go motioned' Sylvie. The group sprang up running low into the woods. But they had been spotted and the stream of bullets from the MG42 scythed through the trees after them.

Panting they tumbled and stumbled down onto the road, Sylvie leading with Pascal right behind her. They were brought up abruptly by the sight of a German motorcycle standing there. There was no sidecar or gun. Just then a German soldier stumbled out of the bushes pulling up his pants. Frozen they all looked each other. Then Sylvie said, 'kill him'. Pascal looked at her in horror. This was just a boy standing before them, dressed in full Wehrmacht uniform with SS flashes on his lapels sure enough, but still a boy, hardly seventeen years old Pascal thought. He looked again at Sylvie. 'He is just a child' Her face was taught. 'He is the Boche- they shouldn't get children to fight their war' she said 'young ones grow up to be old ones; he is a despatch rider; kill him we can't take prisoners'

Pascal unshouldered the Bren and pointed it at the boy whose face became one of dreadful terror, his eyes pleading for his life, his hands were held high in the air. He started whimpering. Pascal clicked off the catch, held the gun tight and pressed the trigger. A burst of three shots knocked the boy flat on his back. Sylvie immediately dragged the boy into the bushes and said 'quick, any Germans following would have heard those shots – lets go'. On they ran for an hour, back the way they came, to the farmhouse. No one else was there. After half an hour Sylvie became worried. 'I hope the others didn't run into a German patrol' she said. 'Normally they wouldn't do a sweep unless there were fatalities then they would be out for hostages and revenge'

'But there was a fatality, the boy,' said Pascal. He was shaking now. Sylvie poured him a brandy; 'So it's the first time you have killed anyone; you will get used to it, you always remember the first, like your first love affair. There will be a lot more killing before this war is over' she said.

Twenty-Three

HAPPY FAMILIES

Yvette couldn't wait for Wolfgang to finish his shift. She was quietly playing a bit of Bach that she had been practicing. Her mother had a sharp tongue when needed and chastised her for playing German music. Yvette retorted "it's beautiful music and nothing to do with what's happening to us now. It was composed a long time ago before Hitler and his gang came to power and corrupted our leaders so that they became puppets of the Reich and us the slaves."

Wolfgang arrived and they all had supper. Yves kept looking at his mother with the quizzical look that said, "aren't you going to tell her, or am I?" His mother shook her head. After supper Wolfgang said 'Things are hotting up. We have been placed on six hours' notice to move. Maybe it's a practise but if real I could be gone with my unit very suddenly. I want to say how happy I have been here in this family. You have all been very kind. I wish things were different and maybe soon they will be. I don't have the great faith in the war that my senior officers have but I have to do my duty'

Yvette touched him on the shoulder and said that she was touched by his kindness and ability, 'You have brought lovely music into this house and that surpasses all the horror and cruelty around us. I wouldn't have learned any Bach without you.' She gave him a kiss on his cheek.

Twenty-Four

YVETTE AND WOLFIE PICNIC

'Tomorrow I want to take you to a special place toward Leojac,' she said' where a running stream sings a concerto of its own against the background of the woods. But it's about 2 kilometers away and I don't have a pass for this area'

'That sounds a lovely idea' Wolfgang said 'and being Sunday I do have some time off as long as there is no call up so I will take you my field wagon; but you must meet me at the edge of town because you would get into trouble if seen with a German officer in town. Let's say 1130 at the crossroads on the small D70 road to Greenbriers'. I will have the pass for you. Don't be late!'

Yvette trembled with excitement. What was she doing? She knew this wasn't right, but she was overcome with an emotion that she knew was stupid; she had lost Pascal and suddenly Wolfgang might also be taken away from her. Her little world would collapse. How could she go on without a dream to help her day get bye?

The next morning Yvette didn't tell her mother

except to say she was going out for a walk. She carefully walked to the East side of town. She was dressed in a white blouse and black blazer on top of a blue skirt with white socks and blue walking shoes. She sported a plaid beret at a cheeky angle. She got several wolf whistles as she deliberately sauntered along so as not to raise interest, but she created the opposite effect. She looked smart and it was a rare image for townsfolk to see; and especially the off-duty German soldiers who sang to her as she walked, something about someone called *Lili Marlene*, but although she didn't know the song, its lilting melody cheered her up. It was already warm, a beautiful April day.

As she turned left up Rue Amade to skirt the parc, she froze. She was sure she could see Terri, rabbit girl, and a man she didn't recognise, crossing the street up ahead. They hadn't seen her, and she let them disappear. But she knew she must not be recognised. Maybe it was stupid to wear what she was wearing; maybe old jeans and a sweater would be more appropriate; maybe she should have dressed in something more mature and sober for Wolfgang. She quickened her gait, but it took another ten minutes before she arrived at the crossroads of Avenue Leojac and Rue Rueramierou. There was no one there. Where was Wolfgang. She couldn't risk being picked up by a German patrol. She crouched down behind a big oak tree, trying to be as small as possible. Five minutes passed then she heard a vehicle coming from the south. The field wagon came into view and much to her relief there was Wolfgang. He pulled up, got out and walked round to open the door for Yvette. 'Bonjour, you look very pretty today' he said. Yvette smiled and got into the basic army vehicle. "Right, where are we going?' he said. 'Well, it's by a beautiful lake called Lac du Tarn along the D70 about five miles." Of course, she thought with a sudden pang in her stomach, that wasn't so far when she and Pascal went there because they went on horses across the farmland and through the woods. That had cut off a big triangle. They came to a roadblock. They stopped. The soldier looked at the Captain and briefly at his papers and then asked Yvette for hers. She produced her papers and the travel carnet Wolfgang had prepared for her.

'She's with me' Wolfgang said.

'We can't be too careful because of the terrorists, they are getting increasingly bold,' said the guard. With that he saluted and waved them through.

'The area around the lake is now a restricted area, open only to Germans; we believe there are many Maquis living up in the hills so now we have more patrols' Said Wolfgang as they approached a small road off to the right.

'Go up here and stop when you get to the top,' said Yvette. They parked between the trees beside a stream looking down at the lake.

'It's beautiful here' said Wolfgang as he parked the kubelwagon pointing slightly down so that they could see the view; the hillside was alive with flowers and plants cascading down, covering the small rocky crevices; primroses and violets still carpeted the banks of the stream with daffodils and one or two wild orchids cushioned with ferns. Yvette pointed to the clump of flowers bordering the trickling water and said 'look at those lovely lilies, the freshness of the white petals and the bright yellow stamens waiting for the insects and bees to come and spread rebirth all around us; Look closely Wolfgang, you can see our national Fleur-de-lys.

Three petals bound together at the base, almost like the coat of arms of old. May is the best months to see spring wildflowers such as cowslips, wood violets and lily of the valley in bloom'.

C'mon – let's get out and taste the sweet water that has probably travelled all the way down from the lower Pyrenees.

They jumped out of the wagon and lay face down on the ground, cupping the water in their hands and sipping. It was cold. It was scintillatingly fresh. It was full of flinty minerals. And it was elusive, slipping through their fingers. A thrush was singing above their heads in the conifer trees, distracting the squirrels from finding the nest.

'Well, my little schoolgirl, you are getting poetic!' But he was touched at her friendliness and his words didn't come easily. He went to the wagon and brought out a bottle of schnapps, bread and sausage. 'Let's eat our little picnic' he said. They lay on the cushion of flowers, and he broke the bread and cut slices of sausage to go with it. He opened the bottle and offered her a drink. She took a swig feeling very grown up; possibly too much, but although it was a bit rough, it warmed her through and through. He took a bigger swig. They ate the picnic and they both took another swig from then bottle. The air was still, the silence between them was very loud, broken in the background by the tumbling stream. "we are so lucky to catch the end of the spring flowering,' said Yvette. 'it's as though we have entered a sacred rockery where time stands still.'

"so why have you brought me here, this place must mean something special to you,' said Wolfgang.

Yvette turned over and lay on her back. 'Wolfie", she used his colloquial name that was intimate and warm. 'Wolfie, I have a big request to ask of you' she said looking up at the blue sky between the trees and then turning to look at him and buoyed up with confidence by the schnapps, and with all the intensity she could muster as though that would give more gravitas to the request that she felt her silent brown eyes alone were trying to say aloud to him.

'So, tell me Yvette' he said.

'A very good friend of our family was suddenly taken away by the gestapo two weeks ago. He was an honest farmer, even half German I think from Alsace. No one knows why or where he is. It would be a big favour if you could make enquiries, please Wolfgang, you did promise to enquire a few weeks ago' she said.

'Did I? Well, the gestapo is a law unto themselves; even we have to be careful of them. They may have suspected him of helping the Maquis, hiding weapons, or even hiding Jews. What's his name and which farm was he from"

'His family name is Pascal Frederic, and he is from the farm called Ferme de Peuplier because it has a drive with poplar trees. It's about a kilometer outside the town boundary on the D70.'

'Isn't that the road we drove down on the way here?' said Wolfgang.

Yvette blushed inwardly. That was a silly mistake she thought. Now he knows it's my friend, not just the family.

'Yes, that's right, we would have past it I think' she said. "Wolfie, I think I know you are a good man and will help, won't you?'

'There's a difference between thinking something and knowing it' said Wolfgang. 'You think I am a good man, but you have to remember I am a German soldier who has sworn allegiance to Hitler and the Reich, so you can't possibly know me. Sometimes I don't even know myself except that I am following orders. Good or bad doesn't come into it.'

Yvette suddenly looked so sad that Wolfgang pulled her to him and said 'Don't be sad; I will do everything I can to find out what's happened to your friend' he said with a huge smile, his face close to hers. It could have been Pascal lying with her she thought. In the heat of the moment, she kissed him on the cheek. The sudden warmth of her body now close made him forget everything about the war; his hands started caressing her deeply. Yvette suddenly felt a surge of electricity pulse through every nerve, opening the buttons on her blouse, and as he slid inside her, gave herself up to happiness; if he would help her find Pascal then she would let him do anything to her even just for his pleasure and reward. After all, he might be gone tomorrow and helping him find that pleasure, even for a few moments against the horrors that would await him was little reward. Saving herself for Pascal was now confusingly abandoned in her frenzy to find him. And against all her mothers' warnings that there was plenty of years ahead to bear the babies of France, she fell into the pleasure of the moment. The bright sunshine enveloped them like a warm moist blanket and carried them both away deep into their inner selves.

Twenty-Five

STARVATION NOW THE ENEMY

APRIL 19TH FULL MOON 96%

General Lammerding called his senior officers together. 'The training is not going fast enough, and the guerrilla activity is increasing in the Dordogne. You have to increase the patrols. Tonight, is a good opportunity for enemy air drops to be made, so look to your informers and gather all the data on the likely zones for both parachute supplies and light aircraft landings. I want the men to be increasing their vigilance and arrests. In the likely event of an invasion by the allies in the next few months, it will either come in the Pas de Calais or Brittany. Their armies are being built up in England. OKW has informed us that when the invasion comes, their assessment is that the French population will rise up in battle against us. So, a plan is being made to abandon all German held territory south of the Loire. This communique is from General Keitel head of OKW. Clearly it is top secret because if the resistance get to hear about it then the situation in the south will collapse. We are here to fight armies, not civilians or terrorists who rise up in revolt. It would be like swatting flies. I have had experience of that in Russia when the insurgents got behind our lines. So, gentlemen, stop living like kings in this beautiful part of France where there are millions of human mosquitos wanting to kill us, get out there and swat these mosquitos, get your patrols out there and let's snuff out any help for the allies.'

Claude and Jenny had been busy going from farm to farm to train the Maquis in small arms and explosives. At each farm they were asked do you have any food to sell us? The farms had been stripped of food; the whole of France was like a once beautiful bountiful orchard whose trees had been pruned bare and all the apples and pears shipped off to Germany.

'They have pitifully little to fight with considering the might of that powerful army camped on their doorstep. Small arms are all very well in close encounters, but the Germans are skilled in manoeuvres, with tanks. They always have been a mobile army said Jenny'

'That's why they cannot engage the *Das Reich*, they can only disrupt communications, railways and bridges; and then slink away. Any confrontation will end in disaster,' said Claude.

At one farm they met a band of particularly aggressive Maquis.

'Look' said the leader; they have taken all the horses and grain; we have no food left; we are all slowly starving.' Claude didn't take the bait; this group of maquisards were the *FTP - Franc Tireurs and Partisan*, a totally communist organisation group with a different agenda; the Allies were not their priority; the communists had long harboured hatred towards the middle class in France and wanted to not only attack them and get the Germans and Vichy out of France; they wanted to overturn the French establishment and install a communist government in France after the war. However, Claude knew they were the most effective guerrilla group in France numbering some five thousand in the southwest and maybe a hundred thousand all over France and in their fight against the Germans, Claude knew they were good and that was why they had to be supported, politics aside. In fact, most French people lived alongside the Germans peaceably, taking their money and were grateful for peace and good order they brought to the streets and saw the maquis as bands of brigands disturbing the peace. The maquis were getting innocent people shot; they killed Germans then slinked off into the woods and the Germans took revenge against the ordinary folk.

'I will ensure that you get more supplies of arms and weapon for close combat, also plastic explosive for sabotage. In fact, I will get you the plans for the Sten gun and how to make it here; they are very simple guns made from pressed steel and can be made very cheaply' Claude said

'That's good – when will more arms arrive, as you can see, we don't have much here," said the leader. 'And also, we need tobacco and cigarettes to keep the morale up with our young men, its important as food. You have no idea how difficult it has been to raid army barracks and supply depots just to find enough camp beds for the group, so morale needs to be kept high. Cigarettes are important'

'We will contact London tonight' said Jenny and with that they left and returned to the farm.

That night Jenny made the usual contact with London and received an immediate answer which read; 'package already en route two days arrival. You will receive double the last'

That's great said Claude but a bit mysterious; 'why are they stepping up shipments? Maybe something is in the air like the invasion' he mused

Over the next ten days they received three drops. The maquisards were delighted. It posed a problem of where to store the goods as so much was buried around farmhouses.

Twenty Six

LE DÉBARQUEMENT

TUESDAY MAY 1ST 1944 97% FULL MOON

"Ici Londres ! Les Français parlent aux Français …"
Les sanglots longs- from the beginning of June 1944, the Allies inundated the network with messages. On 1 June alone, over 200 messages were sent, making it clear to those listening that something was in the works.

'Des violons

De l'automne'

Per Arthur Symons' translation: "When a sighing begins / In the violins / Of the autumn-song".

'Molasses tomorrow will bring forth cognac.'

"Jean a une longue moustache" translated as "John has a long moustache."

The Germans wrongly believed that these lines were addressed to all Resistance circuits in France, and that when the next three lines were broadcast it would mean that invasion would follow within forty-eight hours," But the lines were directed to a single Resistance

112

circuit, named Ventriloquist, working south of Orléans, instructing it to stand by for the next three lines, which would be the signal for it to carry out its railway-cutting tasks — in conjunction with the Allied landings."

Then, on June 5, to signal that sabotage efforts should begin, the next three lines were sent:

'Blessent mon coeur
D'une langueur
Monotone',

At last, they were coming.

Twenty Seven

INVITATION TO LUNCH

n Baker Street Maurice Buckhart in F department had received a message from Allied Strategic Command; it was now time to alert the French nation that the invasion was coming.

The days had become sunny and warm. It was truly spring, and the countryside looked bountiful with its growth of new trees and pastures although there weren't many animals left to enjoy the grazing, hardly a cow, some goats and a few sheep here and there. The French were eating everything under their noses. Fortunately, flour was still available to make bread although only baguettes were now being made as there was not enough for the traditional large wheel or moule. Even the baguettes were getting shorter, still fat at 2.4 inches but not the usual 26 inches long, more like 20 inches now, and certainly less than the normal nine ounces in weight. 'We have to share out what we can' said Madam Bezier.

Rudi at Café Flaubert had increased business now with the fine weather. He put more tables and chairs outside and the Germans flocked to his little café to enjoy an ersatz coffee and a cognac of which there still a plentiful supply. The warm 30c sunshine made everyone happier. Terri met her usual contacts in the café to pass on the latest information. Even Yvette stopped by to see if there was any more news of Pascal. No one knew anything.

'Why don't you come to our house for lunch tomorrow?' said Terri to Yvette. "Your little brother knows the way, but don't bring him. I have something to discuss with you in private'.

At the signal box Raoul and Hans were very chatty even with the new guard overseeing them. 'Have you seen how the young girls of the town are flaunting their pretty summer dresses at the young German soldiers' said Hans, 'reminds me of when I was young!'

Raoul replied 'It will get them into trouble, teasing like that'

'Ach, it is the spring, and all young people should enjoy the love in the air' said Hans 'and you should know that the French girls are sleeping with the Germans not just for money, they find them young, handsome, virile; they have no French men around so it's only naturel'

'Well, said Raoul, 'the reason there are no Frenchmen around is that they have all been rounded up and taken off to Germany to work, or they have just escaped to the hills and join the maquisards. It's your own fault that the terrorists are now growing so strong; what would you do, faced with the STO (Service du Travail Obligatoire) A choice between transportation to work as slave labour in German factory or freedom in the countryside with the maquis? You know Hans, maybe you are a romantic at heart but there's nothing romantic about what is happening here in Montauban. Rumours are that the Gestapo has requisitioned a private mansion, the Hôtel de Vezin, located at 3 Faubourg du Moustier in Montauban under which they have a torture chamber. It's not romantic at all.'

'Well Raoul, 'The German army is falling back everywhere, I heard that the Americans are nearly in Rome, the Russians have taken back the Crimea and that the devastation on route of nine of German infantry and trucks in Italy is immense, so they the German army is being driven back everywhere. The war is lost for Germany,' Said Hans. 'It's not so much our army; land battles are one thing, but the war is being lost in the air. We have no Luftwaffe left, and our U-boat fleets are virtually destroyed

'Yes, I think so too, but then you have this *Das Reich* division of twenty thousand men here in Montauban all geared up for a fight. But there is no army to fight here, just maquis'

The alarm bell rang in the signal box; Raoul pulled the home signal to green and the answering whistle of the one train a day, the 1030 am from the coastal town of Perpignan could now be heard coming into the station. Although the rail network was being constantly disrupted either by sabotage or allied bombing, the Germans still managed to run a skeleton passenger schedule amid the priority military traffic.

Twenty Eight

ENOUGH TO EAT

The relationship between Yvette and her mother had improved; Yvette's music had come on leaps and bounds under Wolfie's tuition, although the time he spent in the house was very limited. He was now out training hard with his tank crew. They had to know how to repair everything on the tank, so first they stripped it down to study how each part fitted to the other. His new Panther tank weighed over forty tons, powered by the same Daimler-Benzes diesel engine as fitted to the new Tiger tanks but the Panther was much lighter and more able to traverses rough ground. The Interleaved overlapping rubber rimmed track wheels were sometimes a nuisance as rocks could get trapped between then and track replacement was practised over and over. Also, the transmission kept failing; a transmission built for a 30-ton tank is inadequate when the tank is now 45 tons. Wolfie would have preferred to see the gears running in an oil bath but there was little oil available.

Wolfie said to Wilhelm, "you know how we used to

have properly machined complex gears, the machines have all gone so we are left with straight cut gears' 'Ach it's not just that' said Wilhelm, the quality of the steel is all shot, and we are out of alloying elements like molybdenum so it's a miracle the bloody tank runs at all!' "We just have to make the best of it and make sure we have an engineer gang following our group" said Wolfie. But he was more concerned about the transmission than he cared to admit.

Yves was hardly at home, running around with his friends, running errands for Terri, Rabbit girl, and getting rabbits in return which Yvette now said nothing about, the household happy to have bread and meat on the table. Cheese supplies were non-existent due to a dearth of cows. There was happily still some last year's hard goats and sheep's cheese available.

Yvette was worried about what happened between her and Wolfgang. What if she was pregnant? The awful feeling of the consequences from the towns people and above all her mother kept her awake at night. She managed to put it behind her until next month. Wolfie didn't mention it.

Twenty-Nine

FARMHOUSE SUPPER

MAY 5TH

It was already a hot morning with the promise of more heat, maybe a thunderstorm in the air. Madam la grange was very bubbly because she had news that her eldest daughter had given birth to a baby boy.

'We need more baby boys 'she said, to replace all our boys who have been lost in the war and to make France big and strong again'. Jenny and Claude congratulated her. In recognition Madam la Grange was preparing a big supper for the whole family to come that evening and to share in the celebrations. Jenny and Claude were invited.

'In the meantime,' she said 'I have a message from Le Rat, he wants to meet you here tomorrow morning, 10 o'clock he has an important message from Andre Malraux and wants to take you to him. He will bring a guide; The guide will be helpful, especially to evade the Germans'.

That night a party of six sat down to a scrumptious wild boar supper. Madam la grange introduced her two daughters, Amelie and Rosemary, the new mother; her little newly born daughter whose name was to be Valerie. Jenny was surprised that the mother and baby were out of hospital so quickly. 'ah well said Rosemary I did not give birth in a hospital what luxury that would be, no I gave birth at home with my friend to help and it was not a long Labour only three hours, little Valerie wanted to come into the world quickly although it's not a very happy world at the moment I acknowledge that'

'Well congratulations' said Jenny 'I guess you must be brought up tough down here'. 'No, it is usual' said Rosemary 'bear in mind most people down here all peasants who work in the fields and the mother has to be prepared to put down the scythe when cutting the corn. I'm lucky to have friends but I have seen women give birth in the shade under the apple tree; I've seen that done many times before. The two husbands Eric and John were very talkative describing how they got special treatment from the Germans in return from giving them the best meat, mainly pigs of course, there was a no big joints of beef available anymore those were all gone.

Claude listened and then asked Derek 'are all the Germans from the *Das Reich* division?' 'well yes they're the only ones now in the town as far as I can see the old soldiers have been shipped off somewhere else who knows where they've gone and there's much more increased activity. The soldiers talk of excessive and demanding training even with live ammunition, but they say they don't have too much of that, so the training also has to be with blank rounds. they say that the situation is bad especially around Bergerac where there have been many maquisards' attacks and of course many reprisals. Here we are safe and fortunate to be in Montauban. However, we still have to be very careful because of this the gestapo is increasing its surveillance of everyone in the town and we have many people here who are gathering information and then sending it to the maquis"

"well said Claude as a wine merchant from Bordeaux I don't have much interest except that I hope the war ends soon and then I can get back to seeing all my loyal customers normally, however if there was any interesting information about what the *Das Reich* plans are I will be pleased to hear them just out of curiosity you understand'

'of course 'said Derek 'in return for a fine bottle of Bordeaux that's no problem. perhaps if you want to know a little more there is one contact that I have who is very active in the town; I think she has a lucrative business in selling rabbits on the black market. I don't know her name, but I understand she is often at the cafe and sometimes John and I go down to the cafe in our break time and see her there; very pretty girl, it's amazing what you can learn'

'So, said Claude what is the disposition of the people here in Montauban' 'they're all fed up but extremely nervous about what the *Das Reich* division is going to be doing; they're all very hungry and bored. It wouldn't take much for the Germans to push them over the top and create a mutiny or rebellion, in fact the whole countryside might rise up in an armed uprising'

'I hope not' said Claude 'rumour has it that the allied invasion will be coming soon, and it will be the very worst thing that the population could do is to rise up in rebellion, for the *Das Reich* it would just be like swatting flies, they are here for a far more significant purpose and swatting flies.'

After all the pork with vegetables and madame's apple tart had been consumed with copious amounts of wine, the Brandy was brought out and the Calvados. Claude actually preferred Calvados; Brandy tended to give him a headache whereas Calvados based on apples was a little gentler but still had the desired effect being very alcoholic.

At just after 9:00 o'clock John and Eric got up saying that they had to go back the quiet way because the curfew was now in operation. Rosemary and Amelie said their goodbyes and Claude and Jenny watched them all go out the back door and start walking down a trail through the woods back to the town. Claude and Jenny helped Madame LaGrange clean up and do the washing up. 'You have a lovely family' said Claude to Madam la Grange. 'Yes, I am lucky I am fortunate somebody is smiling on them but as a family unit the Germans leave them alone because they must have their pork and John and Eric are expert of giving their officers the best cuts of all from the abattoir.

Thirty

LES SANGLOTS LONGS, DES VIOLONS, DE L'AUTOMNE

MAY 6TH 1944

The next morning Le Rat was there at 10:00 o'clock sharp and he had with him a Shepherd to guide them to the meeting with Andre Malraux. "We go to the commune of Albefeuille Lagarde, about ten kilometers northwest of Montauban in Tarn-et-Garonne where Andre has installed himself in an old chateau, with his band of maquisards. Our shepherd friend will guide us through the woods; he knows where the best places are to cross the main highway which is brimming with German columns. They set off on foot. Jenny stayed behind. Claude knew that the best weapon and agent could have is luck; and if he was caught, Jenny could inform London. He also knew that if unlucky to be captured and tortured, he had to give snippets of information only; things the

Germans would already know. He would have to hold out for forty- eight hours, the time needed for any circuit to be alerted and scattered. That was all that was expected because everyone gave in eventually.

After two hours they arrived at the Chateau, the shepherd said it had been built around 1741 in the reign of Louis XV, Louis the beloved so called but Claude didn't think there was very much beloved about a king who drained the coffers of France to fight unnecessary wars and his reign reduced France to complete poverty and led eventually to the French Revolution. The Chateau was well away from any main rd in beautiful countryside and had extensive coach houses and barns surrounding the small targeted castellated building with a magnificent entrance hall. They were shown into a large room with an ornate desk behind which sat Andre Malraux and a large black Pyrenean dog which barked and was introduced as Albert

'Ah Claude he said how nice to see you again, come and sit down and with a welcoming gesture his arm he swept them both into two comfortable chairs facing the table. The Shepherd had gone to the kitchen to get something to drink whereas for Claude and le Rat, Andre had a flask of water and some cognac ready. The dog licked Claude's boots.

'By the way, we are now known as the 'Symposium' circuit so if you hear that name on the radio, it's us. Now, when is the invasion going to come' said Andre 'we cannot store anymore weapons our coach houses are full of them and we will explode sometime.

'They get practice using them and want to drive the

Bosch out of France' Claude said. 'Andre, I would think you are very vulnerable here after all 10 kilometers down the road is a large army and I'm very surprised that the Germans have not used this for one of their command centres'

'Ah it is too run down for them, there is no heating, the roof leaks, the kitchen is a mess, why would they come and live in a wreck when they can live in much better chateaus and hotels?

Besides the Germans do not bother us very much; they only venture out in daylight and then only with full armed guards; it is almost a case of live and let live, if we don't do anything to them, they don't do anything to us. In fact, we now own the south of France; we can travel anywhere without hindrance. Here below the Loire the Germans have given up'

'Well Andre to answer your question I believe the invasion will be coming very soon. As you know we have been told to listen to messages on the 1st, 2nd, 15th and 16th of every month. Already personal messages have become more frequent and the one last week was an advice that the debarqements will be soon, the message was 'Molasses tomorrow will bring forth cognac' they must do it on the night of the full moon and as you know the moons are becoming fuller and fuller recently. I should think it will happen within the next 30 days, but be assured that we will let you know as soon as we hear the code name to be given for the invasion to begin. I am aware of my own personal code 'the dice are on the carpet' and the general one will be the first three lines, an extract from the poem by Paul Verlaine's "Chanson d'automne" – Les sanglots longs, Des violons, De l'automne" which will mean 15 days to go. When the next three lines are broadcast it will be within 48 hours.'

'good said Andre, my message is 'jean has a long moustache" I have at least 5000 men waiting for that message and my plan is to block the main Rd to Bergerac through which I know the *Das Reich* division will have to pass if it is going North. In fact, I shall block the road just outside Sarlat, in fact at the village of Vitrac but on the other side, not the port of the Vitrac as they come up the D 46 from Gordon or Domme'

'I don't think they'll come that way at all said Claude, it's much too narrow and twisty, they'll go straight up the main Rd up the D822 Celiac and Brive'

'no, no, no' said Andre 'they will want to split up their forces in case of air attacks by the jazbos; south of the Loire they are safe from allied aircraft, but they'll probably split their artillery and infantry away from their tanks although they leave some infantry with the tanks of course we'll see but anyway I shall mount the barricades' he said with a triumphant grin. 'Already here in the Dordogne and Correze it is virtually open season on any German. Even in Toulouse, the German barracks have netting to prevent grenades being thrown at them. We are in control. We have even implemented our own rationing card system for the population, the farmers must sell everything to the maquisards now, not to the Germans.'

'Anyway, come and see our supply of arms, we had six tonnes dropped to us the other night, we had to get the farmers oxen to come and pull the crates in, there were so heavy without the help of the oxen'

They all went to the barn and there were stacked up crates and crates of new weapons, there were also some First World War rifles and a First World War light machine gun standing against the wall but when Andre pried open the casks Claude could see stacks of sten guns and in another crate bren guns wrapped in oily parchment, and in another crate stocks of gammon bombs and explosives.

'You have enough arms here to arm the whole of France' said Claude but make sure you know who you give them to and that they have training and how to use these things'

'Yes', said Andre some of the young lads here like to be seen to pose with a gun but they don't know how to use it, how to clean it out or load it or even how to fire it, probably most of our men are young who have just tried to escape but we will improve their fighting ability with your help. You know the weapons, so I am counting on you to train them. So please train as fast as possible'. With that Claude le rat and the Shepherd man decided that it was time to leave, it was now getting late in the afternoon and although the sun was still shining hot, they knew that they needed to get back to their farm without delay'

It took them twice as long to get back to the farm because they could hear vehicles, probably German vehicles on the roads 'they're putting out patrols' said Le rat 'and we must be careful'. In fact, back at the farm Madam LaGrange did not have good news. I've just had a message from my son Eric at the abattoir she said the Germans are planning a sweep tomorrow and we must hide you and Jenny somewhere else you can't stay here.

Thirty-One

CLAUDE AND JENNY ESCAPE ANOTHER SEARCH PARTY

MONDAY MAY 8 FULL MOON 100% ILLUMINATION

The next morning Claude and Jenny had moved out into the Woods into a tent, Madame la grand had given them some food so all they could do now was wait for the sweep to be over. Jenny had all the gear with her, the heavy transmitter and the 12volt car battery, fully charged but she knew there was very little chance of success of transmitting from inside the thick copses of the woods. They then heard vehicles coming up to the farm. Madam LaGrange was busy as usual cleaning and sweeping and tidying. In marched a young German captain and five men. 'Bonjour Madame' he said, 'we want to search your premises, we believe you are hiding English Flyers here.'

'Well of course you can search Captain, you have been

here before and know your way around'. said Madame LaGrange 'there's no one here except me but you're welcome to have a look and would you like a drink in the meantime? the captain said no then he turned to her and said told his men to conduct the search. 'I have to ask you why you've got such a big kitchen and so much food here, do you run a side-line on the black market?' 'I actually do cook for a number of people, they are the small farmers around here who have got nothing left, all their animals have gone but they do shoot the odd wild boar for me, and I cook that and cut it up and send it to them that's why I've got so much food on the grillage now, they're like my extra family because my family is not here'

'Where is your family?' said the captain 'well my two sons work at the abattoir and you must know them because they supply you with lots of pork and they have married two lovely French wives and now I have a grandson as well, two weeks old.' 'You are very lucky' said the captain back in Germany I have a family but I haven't seen them for six months and they are in a very bad part which is bombed every night by the Americans and the English so that is why we must find these English Flyers who have been shot down and are now working their way down to Spain. Of course,' he said, 'if we do find anybody they will be taken away and you will be shot for harbouring enemies of the Reich Madam". Madam smiled and the captain smiled but she was very easy and relaxed. She could tell that these men were ordinary Wehrmacht soldiers and not SS. They looked a poor bunch of old men. 15 minutes later the search party came back and said that they had discovered nothing suspicious "okay said the captain but you must search the woods as well, go.' Madam interrupted and said 'Captain, for your own safety I would advise against that. This area has many maquisards and you could easily run into fifty of them camped up there somewhere.' The corporal nodded, 'Herr Captain, I think Madam is right. We are no match for fifty brigands. We have accomplished our task and can report back that the farm is clear;' The Captain hesitated. 'thank you very much for your time, Madam, sorry to disturb you but if you do see anybody, please contact us as I said if you hide anybody you will be in trouble, and we shall burn the farm down. Now I now know why you cook for so many people' he said with a half-smile. But he knew that her sons provided meat for him, and his men so let and let live he thought. With that they got into their halftrack and moved off down the road. Madame LaGrange heaved a sigh of relief; while it was true she was cooking for the bands of maquisards, she was in fact also cooking for some of the farmers who had lost their sons to work in Germany and were unable to manage their farms so they had all clubbed together, they brought her vegetables, they brought her meat, rabbit and venison and wild boar so, she was like a restaurant in the woods for dozens of people but she loved the cooking and it kept her busy and it kept her safe, for the moment. When Claude and Jenny returned, she told them the story. 'are there really fifty maquisards in the woods near here?' asked Jenny. 'I have no idea' said Madam la grange with a smile, 'but it worked. The ordinary Germans who were here fear the population rising up against them, so they don't take unnecessary chances!'

Thirty-Two

RAID ON THE PHARMACY

MAY 10, 1944

Pascal was relaxing in the sunshine outside the shack in the woods in where the band of maquisards were camped. Pascal couldn't help thinking of his farm and of his little girlfriend Yvette, but Sylvie had more things on her mind. she was in deep discussion with Hugo and Gaspard whilst the other members of the band we're cleaning their weapons that they had acquired more of in recent weeks, stolen from the Germans and some parachute drops but not many of those came their way. Sylvie then said to gather round, she wanted to discuss the plan of the next operation with everyone. The train attack had been a great success particularly as the line have been blocked for six hours and it took more than the usual German efficiency to repair because said Sylvie 'I know they had to bring in a crane from Poitier to lift the engine off the track. Now I have a request from a lot of people around here people running farms and, in the villages, they're running out of medical supplies and the only people that have the medical supplies are the Germans but as luck would have it, there is a small medical Depot in Montmorillo, 5 kilometers from our hideout'. Theo Jean and Lucian knew that this was true because some of their very own families were suffering from lack of proper drugs. 'So' said Sylvie 'we need to establish how many Germans are guarding that supply Depot' 'I will go and check' said Hugo and two hours later he came back with the news that there were six Germans there. 'ah' said Victor 'so where has the whole Garrison gone? Maybe they've been recruited to go up Poitier to help mend the railway lines and guard against the saboteurs. The English and American bombing has done a lot of damage to the railroad yards and the tracks, so we won't see them back here for a while. 'So' said Sylvie 'six of them and eight of us, that should be enough for an attack, but we must do it carefully and we have to do it quietly, so we'll go tonight at 9:00 o'clock. Pascal, as you are fluent in German, I want you to lead us in, take this German uniform we've got here, put it on especially the cap and speak to the guard on the door and tell him that that you need sulphur, you need bandages, aspirin, disinfectant, syringes, and morphine for your soldiers and anything else you see that is of value will take it'. They each put on a big rucksack and with the sten guns slung over their shoulders and hand grenades packed into their gillette's they set off for the town. It was dark when they got to the centre of the town hardly a town thought Pascal more like a small village. Sylvie posted Theo, Jean, and Lucian at diverse sections on the roads around where the pharmacy was then Sylvie, Hugo,

Gaspard, Victor all went up to the little store where the supplies were. Pascal knocked on the door, but he could hear singing and broadly brawling noises coming from inside. Maybe the Germans there were drunk, even better but Pascal did not know what kind of infantry had been left behind, if it was seasoned SS that could be a problem. The door was opened by a Corporal in all dressed in ordinary Wehrmacht uniform. 'Yes', he barked, he had a gun in his hand pointing straight at Pascal who was dressed in the uniform of an SS major. 'Stand to attention' said Pascal in his best German 'and put that gun away'. the Corporal stood up straight and raised the Nazi salute 'I'm sorry herr mayor, I did not know it was you'

'Of course, you didn't' said Pascal in a reassuring tone. 'now I need some morphine for one of my soldiers 'ah' said the Corporal 'we have very small amounts of that, but I'll give you what I can spare,' Pascal moved into the inside of the store and the Corporal unlocked the gate behind which where the drawers of medicines. As soon as the Corporal unlocked the gate Pascal brought his gun out and hit him on the back of the head, he went down heavily, then Sylvie Hugo Gaspard and Victor came running in. 'Quiet' said Pascal because next door the Germans were singing and they could hear the beer and the wine being drunk, 'keep quiet and we will be fine,' said Sylvie. They packed as much of the supplies as they could into all of their rucksacks but just as they are about to go Hugo dropped his gun and it clattered to the floor. They stood horrified and then the door opened and now in came a big fat German soldier, he stopped in horror when he saw the band of brigands in front of him, then he raised his gun but before he could do anything Hugo fired his Sten and he fell a big splodgy fat heap on the floor; the singing had stopped, Victor ran forward with his loaded Sten gun and sprayed the room, there were cries and screams of men falling and guns clattering onto the floor, one of the Germans was quicker to respond, he obviously wasn't as drunk as the others and he fired and caught Victor in the doorway with a bullet in his arm before Hugo shot him dead but they weren't all dead, another German appeared from behind a cupboard in the room but before he could level his machine gun Hugo tossed a grenade into the room and shut the door. There was a mighty explosion 'Oh mon Dieu' said Sylvie, 'they will hear that all the way to Poitiers! come on we must go quickly' and with that they all ran out of the store. A shot came down the road 'Oh no said Hugo 'it's the French Milice, 'look they've come from the barracks just down the road, I'd forgotten about them'. there was a spray of bullets splattering the payment on the walls around them. 'Run' said Hugo, 'we will cover you' and he and Gaspard levelled their sten guns and raked the street ahead of them. The others ran. 'come on quickly' said Sylvie 'we haven't got much time to lose'. Victor's arm was bleeding badly so Pascal grabbed one of the bandages and made a tourniquet tight around his arm above the elbow. Jean and Lucian set up a defence and called for Hugo and Gaspard to fall back as they covered the street with withering fire. They all turned and ran but the French Milice started to come running down the street but again Hugo tossed a grenade in that direction, and they all ran for cover. By now they were all clear of the town and running for the Woods, but they knew that the Milice would report this incident to the nearest German Garrison and there would be a patrol along soon, so they had to make haste. They got back to their woodland lair and stuffed the medicines and Pharmaceuticals that they had managed to steal into crates which they then put underneath the hay in the barn.

'Tomorrow', said Sylvie 'we will distribute these to those who need it'. Fortunately, no one had pursued them, but Sylvie knew that the Germans will come the next day or the day after making a sweep through the countryside trying to find out who had stolen their supplies and killed six of their men. That was the more worrying thing and if Hugo hadn't dropped his weapon on the floor making such a clattering noise, they would have been out of there without anybody being hurt at all, still living on the edge was the chance they took.

Thirty-Three

TERRI'S SECRETS AND A TRAP

MAY 10, 1944

Yvette decided it was time to visit Terri who had invited her to lunch at her house. Terri lived about a kilometer into the countryside. Yves said he would take her, so they left the house and walked to the South of the town and into the countryside. It was a lovely hot day, and all the birds were singing, the meadows look beautiful with all the foliage bursting out and the trees and flowers in full bud. They came to the farmhouse where Terri lived and knocked on the door. She answered the door and bid them welcome to come inside, Yvette was surprised how large it was. 'Come and meet my family' said Terri and she took them in to another large room in which there were three boys sitting with an elderly man and an older lady. 'these are my brothers' said Terri pointing to the young men who were probably older than her but looked tough and uncompromising. 'and this is my mother and father', she introduced them, and they all shook hands. The mother had prepared a nice lunch of salad and some ham, she opened a bottle of wine and they all sat down to eat.

'Terri tells me that's your boyfriend has been sent away to Germany 'said the mother, 'that is so sad I hope he is alright, have you heard from him? 'no' said Yvette, her eyes filling with tears, 'I haven't, I don't know if he's dead or alive,' 'are they allowed to write if they are in Germany? 'yes of course' said the old lady 'the Germans encourage it, they like to see that they send a nice postcard saying I'm well, happy and working hard!' 'I'm trying to find out through a contact I have where he is' said Yvette. When they had finished lunch, Terri said that she wanted to have a private word with Yvette, and she suggested that Yves leave and go home but she did give him a big fat rabbit to take back to the house. They went into another room with two big armchairs and a log fire over which hung a big pot of simmering water adding to the already hot day. 'so now'. said Terri 'I need your help', you may know by now that I have Contacts in the resistance, and I have a plan to sabotage the rail waggons full of tanks and armour that is going to be going out of here sometime soon up to the North. We have been told that we must put grinding paste into the grease points of the low-loader waggons so that after a few kilometers the grinding paste locks the wheels and axles tight. I think we can do this at night as soon as we get the password of the news that the allies of landed and the *Das Reich* will be on the move.

'I don't think I can do that said Yvette if we are both caught, we will be shot, and I could not leave my mother all alone. I can't risk that'

'I don't think you have a choice said Terri, 'I saw you meeting that German captain you have stationed in your house, you met him on the outskirts of town then you got into his car and went off somewhere for the whole afternoon, I can only imagine what happened,' said Terri smiling. And besides you seen that my mother and father and my brothers they are Jewish and I'm half Jewish and I cannot risk them being deported. 'but said Yvette even if they are deported, they would only be sent to Germany to work?'

'ha no' said Terri, 'they will be sent to Poland, and nobody comes back from Poland, do you know why they are sent to Poland she asked? They are sent to Poland to be gassed that's why nobody comes back and enough of our people here in France have already been deported but fortunately now the last transport for Poland from Poitier left last week and I think the Germans have other things on their mind for the use of their rail network in this part of France which is being heavily bombed, they will need all the tracks and trains for moving supplies around when the invasion comes'.

'Yvette was shocked and thought hard. She knew she was trapped. She said 'will you give me your promise that you won't tell anybody about my afternoon with the captain? 'Yes, said Terri I give you that promise' 'will you swear to it said Yvette? 'yes, I swear to it because you are seeing my family and you know the risks that I am taking, so now can I trust you and you have to swear that you won't denounce my family to the gendarmes?

'yes, you can trust me said Yvette with a sigh. 'I will not tell anybody about what I've seen here' 'good' said Terri 'now let me show you our barn' they went outside and across the courtyard to a large barn and inside underneath the hay bales Terri opened a trap door; there in the cellar was a family, a family of four Jews. They are in hiding said Terri so if you breathe a word of this they will be taken out and shot by the Germans. We feed them every day mainly rabbit Stew and bread, my brothers go out hunting for rabbits every morning, there are plenty of them especially at this time of year. Yvette was stunned 'so you've been hiding Jews' she said, 'you know that is against the law, you are really an enemy of the Reich'. the words came out far too easily for Yvette, she had been schooled by Wolfe about what was right and what was wrong after all he was a German, and he supported the Reich, but for the second time she swore that she would not reveal anything to anybody. Then Terri moved to the end of the barn where there were crates underneath some loose straw. Terri prised open one of the crates, there were guns packed in. 'We are well armed said Terri but however well-armed we are we are not armed enough to take on the Germans, we just have to do sabotage and if they catch us, we have to fight our way out. We Jews are not going to go quietly anymore. So now you've seen everything about us and if we are betrayed you your mother on your lovely little brother who runs errands for me will be shot. Understood?

'Yes', said Yvette 'that I fully understand but I am afraid I'm not like you Terri, you seem to be able to move like the wind and mix invisibly amongst all the Germans in the town. You don't seem to have a fear in your head at all. The Germans scare me. How are you so brave?

Terri sighed and sat down on the bed of straw with the flies were buzzing around 'well she said I did have a sister who is older than me and older than my brothers and in the early years of the war, she was very active in the resistance which was only a few people at that time and mainly communists. She identified with the communists cause but was a fighter, sadly her circuit was betrayed in 1942 and they took her and 5 others away'.

Yvette now understood that Terri had history, and this is what gave her courage to avenge her sister and protect her family.

They went back to the house where her mother made him a drink of cool lemonade made from the lemons on the farm seasoned with sugar. It was very refreshing and by now Yvette had come to terms with what she had to do when called upon. They all said goodbye with smiles, and Yvette walked back to town. She made a detour to the railway station and the marshalling yards to see if she could have a quick word with Paul or even better with Raoul in the signal box, but the yards were heavily guarded by German troops. She walked on home with her mind racing, on the one hand she wanted to do something to satisfy her burning anxiety for Pascal but on the other hand she had become very fond of Wolfe, who was Pascal in absentia. When she got back home her mother was delighted with the rabbit that Yves had brought, 'look what your baby brother has brought home' she said 'why don't you ever bring something home to eat? some apples would be good if you wander outside of the town into a farm'

'He's not my baby brother' said Yvette 'he's a young

Rascal and he ought to know better than mixing with the resistance.' Now her mother was surprised, 'how is he mixing with the resistance?'

'He runs errands for them, the Germans don't suspect the young schoolboy to be mixed up in that and in any case, he's not doing anything dangerous.

'I wish neither of you would get involved with the Germans, it's bad enough having a German billeted in our house,' said Mama

Yvette said nothing but went and played on the piano a quiet peace that Wolfe had taught her.

Thirty-Four

MAMA CAN I LOVE TWO MEN?

When Wolfe returned that evening Yvette was very quiet and he noticed it but didn't make a big point of it, He simply asked if she had had a lovely day had she been out walking in the sunshine? Yvette didn't answer immediately but then said 'yes, I've been to see a friend of mine who lives South of the town, she has a farm from where we brought back another rabbit for supper. So, I'm afraid you're having rabbit food everyday now because we don't have any other meat. 'Yes, I'm sorry about that' said Wolfe 'but it's the same with our troops, everyday all we have is pork, pork this and pork that.'

'But I thought you loved pork' said Yvette 'it's the national dish of Germany, isn't it?' 'Ach, Yes, it is but you can get fed up of caviar you know if you have it every day' Then Yvette said 'have you heard anymore news about Pascal my old boyfriend?' She almost bit her lip when she said it but events of the last few hours had made her very confused, and anyway Wolfie was her new boyfriend now although she was not going to admit that to everybody.

'No, I've had no news said Wolfe I don't even know if he's working in Germany or in the military or a prisoner or anything so I'm afraid event I cannot help you'. 'Have you any news on when you are going to be moving?' asked Yvette, 'no said Wolfie, 'this is very boring waiting and waiting and my men feel that they have been trained as much as they possibly can, they can now dismantle the whole tank and replace every bit if needed. Our leader general Lammerding has been very busy with Maps and as far as I can see from what I have heard we are looking at Maps of the North of France.' 'Gosh' said Yvette 'isn't that a long way from here? how are you going to get there if that is the place where you're going to go?' 'that is, we don't know if we'll get the rolling stock allocated to us. Anyway, there's nothing for you to bother your pretty little head about and without he gave one of his gigantic smiles which always melted Yvette. 'Well, she said I think I'll go and help Mama with the supper. Play a little music for us Wolfe, something nice and melodic.' Wolfe unbuttoned his tunic and took it off. It was hot. He had had a hot day with the men and their machines. He knew what he told her wasn't exactly true because a lot of his men were new recruits from Rumania, which he was very unhappy about. Anyway, he went and started a piece from Handel.

Yvette talked to her mum about Pascal and asked if it was terrible to love two men? 'What are you talking about? Asked her mum, 'well I'm very fond of Wolfe but you know that really I am in love with Pascal, still in love with him wherever he may be. I can't let that go out of my mind until I know one way, or another is he dead or alive.'

"oh" sighed her mother, 'I was in love with three men at your age, there was the Carpenter the butcher and of course your father, they were all good -looking handsome men big and strong but it depended on the day of the week, on the weather, if I was feeling very bubbly on a Friday there would be your father but on Monday morning he was always very grumpy so my attention turned to the butcher who was always very happy chopping away and singing a song. I don't know where he is now and there is some young lad in the butcher shop who hasn't got anything to cut up. And then when it was raining, I was in love with a Carpenter. I used to go to his workshop and watch his skills at making things, I didn't like it when he was making coffins of course that made me very sad. So, you see Yvette there's nothing wrong with having a different man for everyday in the week after all the men have a different girlfriend every day and sailors have a different girl in every port so it's the way of the world, but you have to be careful because, they become very jealous.

'I wish Pascal was here so the jealousy would surface and show itself' said Yvette 'in a way that would make things easier, I am not saying that I want them to fight over me though, she said hastily. 'Mama can I ask you a personal question?' 'Yes of course' she said. 'Well said Yvette is it wrong to be intimate with a man? I'm not saying I have been but sometimes I do get pangs of desire And I don't know where they're coming from!' 'Ah' said her mother 'they're coming from deep inside you and at your age you're programmed to want to procreate and have children, it is the feeling that will urge you on to go with a man but please do not do that at this moment, at least wait until your father gets back. By the way is there anyone in the town that you're thinking of right now someone you cast your eye on and smiled to him and he smiled back? that is the way to communicate, with a smile you can say 1000 words in a smile and if you link that to your eyes then it's 2000 words; with that you don't ever have to utter a single word, it's called infatuation because you like a particular way somebody speaks or walks or talks'.

Then, Yvette asked Mama 'is Papa actually in Germany working or has he been taken to Poland?'

'No, he is in Germany' said her mum 'if he was in Poland he would not be coming back, we all know that that is a graveyard for enemies of the Reich'.

'But he's not an enemy of the Reich' said Yvette, 'he is a good worker and I hope he is staying safe. Can I help you with the shopping Mama?' Her mother knew the signs of when her daughter was troubled and she could tell that there were lots of things going around in her head, a struggle here, struggle there being torn in different directions but what she did not know if maybe it was something to do with her hormones, at Yvette's age they were no doubt very rampant. Anyway, busying herself with the food and the preparation for the supper seemed to improve disposition and they sat down to supper. Then Yves returned a few minutes late. 'where have you been said Yvette? "Ah my big sister would like to know everything that I do wouldn't she' retorted Yves 'but I'm not going to tell you.'

'Did you like the farm I took you too today?' Yvette blushed and the blush was noticed by her mother and by Wolfe. 'yes, it was very nice, and I met some lovely people, now don't ask me anymore questions I'm just going to enjoy the food'. That night in bed she was very uncomfortable, she had opened the window as far as it would go but only hot balmy air hung there, it didn't move she felt like an animal in a cage and that a huge blanket had been thrown over the cage stifling any opportunity for air to come in. Maybe there would be a thunderstorm she thought that would clear the air but all through the hot night no thunderstorm, none came, and she woke in the middle of the night, unable to sleep plagued by the thought of the Jewish family at the farm being sent to Poland. She knew nothing of Poland, was there a tribe of Troglodytes there that gobbled people up? She thought it sounded a very dark place. Then fitfully she fell back to sleep, and in the early hours, she dreamed of two husbands, one who could farm and one who could play beautiful music and they got involved in a competition, trying to find her from up the mountain. The music maker went up the mountain and tried to play music to entice her to go further up the mountain beyond where she had gone to pick flowers. The farmer stayed below with the horses, calling her to come down and ride with him but Yvette could see that she wasn't up a mountain, the husbands were wrong but were both mesmerised by the mountain, it seemed to be calling for music and when it didn't hear any it became angry and suddenly erupted and showered the fields below with the music maker and lots of soldiers tumbling down the mountains.

Thirty-Four

AXLE BEARINGS

MAY 15, 1944

Madam la grange had a meeting with Claude and Jenny to say 'I heard from town that the Germans have brought in much better surveillance equipment to track radio transmissions, so it is unsafe to stay in one place all the time. Think where you can go.' Claude had been dreading this moment because he knew that transmitter operators had to keep moving from safe house to safe house to avoid pinpointed detection. 'Thank you, Madam, I appreciate the problem. When we need to transmit, we will go away from the farm'. The next scheduled transmission was tomorrow night so they would have to make other plans. His job for the next two days was to help train the maquis members of the Symposium circuit for Andre Malraux. They were scattered in various locations, so it involved a courier coming to Claude to give them the addresses. Five or six members at a time. He set off to the first address about a mile away and went through the usual drill of showing how to handle a Sten gun, clean and oil it, how to clear jams (which were a frequent hazard), loading and target practice. The Sten made a racket of a noise at any time so deep in the woods was the answer. Then basic wiring techniques for the plastic explosives, using live detonators and empathising all the time the careful steps so that no one blew their hand off. They were a casual bunch who had no field craft training, but their enthusiasm made up for that.

Raoul and Hans were as chatting as usual in the signal box. Paul had passed a message to Raoul that he was invited to come to supper at Yvette's house for rabbit pie. Yvette had chosen a night when Wolfie was out on manoeuvres and Yves was staying with a friend. Paul came too. 'This is a very pleasant surprise' he said when they met. Mama ensured that they had the freshest bread and had baked a huge pie of rabbit and potatoes. The wine was poured, they chatted and laughed and then after getting up to speed with the gossip, Yvette asked 'Raoul, how do the grease systems work on the low loaders?' Raoul immediately went very quiet. 'You know I can't tell you that; why? What are you planning to do? Any Cheminot (railway worker) who sabotages rolling stock is shot; a driver did that the other day to his locomotive and when the Germans found out, they threw him live into the engines furnace.' Everyone went very quiet. Yvette broke the silence and quietly said 'Raoul, the invasion is coming soon, probably in the next thirty days, so after France is liberated don't you want to proudly say that you played your part? After all, you won't be involved, others will be, and no one could prove that you gave any information. And it's nothing to do with signals or the signal box. You don't have to tell us, just draw it for us.' Paul poured out three large glasses of brandy. What guts this girl has he thought. Mama was very quiet. After a while, Raoul drew a diagram of the axel bearings and the greasing points and the grease box. 'Swear on your honour that this didn't come from me' he said. After another few brandies he was more relaxed and then came curfew time to go. Yvette gave him a big hug and a big kiss. Paul left with him.

'Now young lady, you had better tell me all about this. I don't want you getting into trouble,' said her mother.

'I was asked by Terri, who I went to lunch with the other day, to see if I could get information about axle bearing oiling and greasing points. That's all. It's nothing to do with me, I have no idea why she wants this information.'

'You have lots of pretty words to say' her mother retorted 'and I hope they are all true but your involvement with this rabbit girl has to stop right here'

Yvette said nothing more and diligently helped her mother with the clearing and washing up. She knew she had upset her mother, but the mutual oaths sworn by her, and Terri were locked deep in her heart. Then later she wrote a note to Terri and enclosed the drawings with an explanation of how it all worked in an envelope. She would get Yves to deliver it tomorrow!

Thirty-Five

A NEW FRIEND COMES WITH WOLFIE

MAY 16, 1944

C laude had found another hut for Jenny to transmit from. Up in the woods behind the farm only accessible by donkey track was a waterproof shepherds hut with a clear line of aerial communication for radio. Due to the terrain, no tracker vehicle could come closer than a mile and while jenny huffed and puffed about the long commute, at least she knew she was safer than in the farm. She just had to make sure the smaller portable batteries were fully charged all the time. There was not much new news over the wire from London; the reports focused on Red Army advances with a few personal messages.

Yves took his sisters message down to the café Flaubert where Rudi was in full flow discussing with a group of Frenchmen the war situation. The air was thick with dense pungent Gitanes smoke. Terri was drinking a coffee and gave Yves a peck on the cheek which made him feel ten feet taller in front of all the others. One man was voicing criticism of England and the bombing of French towns; Rouen had 1500 people killed last week by the English bombers and the sooner the Red Army overran France the better it would be. 'You are just an outright communist, France will never be free if the Reds came in,' said Rudi. Yes, said another, but none of this would have happened anyway except for the Jews and the Masons who originated in England, spread to Europe lost us the first world war and have ruined France. Another man spouted about the maquis and how their stupid sabotage activities amounted to nothing effective except reprisals and those 11 men had been shot in Poitiers for railway sabotage, not ten or twelve but precisely eleven just like German exactness. The Germans at least had brought control and order to France and that we should support them to fight the Red Army and the Americans. A third man, the local bank clerk said 'Let people who are for the Germans fight with the Germans, let people who are for the English and Americans fight alongside them. Me, I am for the French and have no reason to fight!'

This brought loud laughter from all in the café and a smile to Terri's face. 'Typical reactions; yes, people are getting restless and asking 'when will they come' she said referring to the invasion. Then we will know the hurt that is happening now will have been worth it.' Yves was fascinated. He had never heard Terri speak like that in public before and was impressed. Just then a squad of German soldiers came in and ordered coffee and schnapps. One of them posted a notice on the café wall. Everyone crowded round to read. It was a proclamation from General Lammerding.

NOTICE

All inhabitants, particularly Doctors and other care givers, who treat in any way whatsoever wounds caused by firearms or explosives are required to declare the fact without delay to the nearest Feldkommandatur or Kreigscommandatur or to the nearest service of German police, indicating the name and address of the wounded person.

Whoever does not submit to the obligation to declare the wounded persons treated by him will be subject to the severest penalty, to the death penalty, if need be, in accordance with paragraph 27 of the edict of December 18, 1943, concerning the safety of the German. Army (Der Militaerbefehkshaber in Francreich)

Everyone sat down, The German major in charge added 'This also applies especially to English bomber crews shot down. Thank you and good day'. Everyone was quiet.

Rudi passed around a free schnaps to help lighten the mood. He then said, "The French Police and the Milice are very active so be careful. They are doing the dirty work for the Germans and have total powers to be judge and jury. Executions are no longer done by guillotine due to the impracticality of dragging it around everywhere, so people are just shot by the French police instead."

That night Wolfie brought home a friend and introduced him to the family. Yves was impressed, so was Yvette and her mama. 'Wolfie made the introduction; 'this is my best friend Wilhelm. He was recently assigned to my unit, and we are both so happy to see each other again. Wilhelm was in another unit and by luck I found out and asked for a transfer to be made as I need a good radio operator and Wilhelm is the best. We grew up together in the same village and both went to the same school. We were, and still are, like brothers. We trained together in officer school; and the German officer school is the best in the world".

'Ya vuhl" retorted Wilhelm 'six months of solid training in all military aspects, especially leadership"

'Yes, and we went straight to a motorised tank division, the German army is still 80% non-motorised, horse drawn, so we had to learn mechanics whereas the ordinary soldier had to learn about horses!'

With that they both burst out laughing.

Wilhelm was very good looking blond and blue eyed and with a very broad smile worth a thousand francs for a pinup that no doubt could charm the ladies across a crowded room. 'We have drunk many beers and schnaps together' said Wilhelm and I have brought a bottle of apple schnaps for the house so let's drink to "mein gute kameraden.' Yvette brought little shot glasses and they all had a toast to the two friends. Yves spluttered and coughed his way through his', but Wilhelm patted him on the back and encouraged him not to sip it but to down it in one go.

Then Yves asked Wilhelm 'can you shoot anyone you want?'

'No of course not, The answer is no, we couldn't

shoot whoever we wanted. When people volunteered for the SS, they had to undergo a background check to see if they are criminals or have a criminal history. We don't allow criminals in the SS. If a soldier was to mistreat his prisoners or a French person, the SS would send us to trial for it. Ironically, that doesn't include <u>all</u> SS or eastern Europe. There it was different.'

Mama interrupted and brought out some bread and then presented a rabbit pie flavoured more heavier with garlic and mixed with green and red peppers; they all sat down to eat. Yvette was quiet; she could see that there was a great bond between the men who were laughing and joking in German, and she started thinking about which was the stronger bond, men with men or men with women? She would ask Wolfie about that. Wilhelm was exceptionally well mannered, which impressed mama, but she like all the town folk had noticed that all the '*Das Reich*' troops were very polite and did not take any liberties especially with the French girls. They were under strict orders to be on best behaviour, they had been imbued with the message that the French were not enemies but friends. And that they were there to protect them. Yvette was quiet. Mama whispered to Yvette 'am I seeing a little jealousy here? Two lovely young men, even if they are Germans?'

Wilhelm said goodnight and everybody went to bed early, a little drunk.

Thirty-Six

AM I JUST A BIT OF FUN?

MAY 17, 1944, MOON COVER 27%
WANING FROM PISCES TO ARIES

Pascal and Sylvie had struck up more than a relationship, it was now openly carnal. Pascal admired her guts and aura of command. They had lain low since the raid on the pharmacy except for distributing the medicines to very grateful farmers and townsfolk, at least those they knew they could trust. It was a perfect night for moving around with almost no moonlight and the warm nights were perfect for cuddling. The other members of the group took the relationship between the two in their stride; they had been brought up to know that sex was different to love, and they all knew the need for it. Any woman who knew her husband was having an affair would dismiss it as not important; if it lasted too long, she would find a lover, but the physical side of their relationships were secondary to love and could easily be forgiven and forgotten.

The night drops were getting more frequent now and every other night there was a message for a parachutage. All over France the rate of drops increased at the same rate as the bombing. Sylvie had been informed that the rail yards at Poitier were a disaster with more attacks every night; there was a major army logistics and communications hub in Poitiers, part of what was called the Communication Zone (ComZ) and consisting of a logistics headquarters and communications for Abwher and Wehrmacht, with armaments factories on the outskirts. Unfortunately, the collateral damage to civilians also increased. "Over 100 civilians killed last night," said Sylvie. That very evening they had sat on the hill and watched the orange and red lights of the explosions coming from Poitier.

'I'm glad we are not down there' said Sylvie 'and there are more and more young French boys deserting and taking to the hills'

Sylvie and Pascal talked about why the English and Americans were choosing to disrupt so much in that area, true it was about 300 kilometers from Paris and about the same from Caen in Normandy. Was this special for the invasion; did this tell them that the invasion would come to Poitier being equidistant from both?

'Did you hear that they are still running transports from Poitier,' Said Sylvie. Yesterday a survivor of a transport said that 2,500 French maquisards were on a transport for five days into Germany; when it arrived at Dachau, only 1500 were alive. The rest, some 980 had no food or water for days before the loading and none during the transit. It makes me boil with anger that they treat prisoners that way. Pascal was quiet then said, 'what's the best way to hit back at them?'

'Well, half the time we don't know who is doing the arresting, the Milice or the French police. It wouldn't be the Germans; they would deal with what they have been handed. There's a lot of old scores to settle with French traitors.'

Pascal then dropped a thought into the conversation. 'I think that I will try and return home soon; I must go see my parents. The Gestapo won't necessarily recognise me or be on the alert for my return. They will have assumed I'm safely tucked away in the German army, or dead. Maybe a few days more and some more chaos on the roads that will help my 350-kilometer journey. But it's difficult, I have no papers or identity card anymore'

'We can help with those,' said Sylvie 'the more difficult part is transport. Even with papers you can't travel on the train because they are changing the security passes almost daily and most trains are reserved for the army anyway which requires a special ausweis (travel card for non-Germans). Give me two days for new papers'

'Are you pining for the school-girl you told me about, what's her name, Yvette? Will you marry her when this is all over? Chirped Sylvie

'Well, I am sure she would be a good mother and she comes from good solid stock. Sometimes the girls you have fun with aren't the ones you want to marry'

'Am I just a bit of fun?' laughed Sylvie who then poked him in the ribs.

'Look I like you a lot and we do hit it off physically,

but I don't see you as the mother of my children' said Claude 'It's just an animal attraction between you and me; love is different, sometimes love is wanting something you can't have'

Ah, said Sylvie, smoking a cigarette languidly, 'you are a country boy, yet you don't seem to know much about the country life on a rural level. The typical 'Bal du village' (village hop) was only deemed a success for many if it included a quickie in nearby bushes. And I know of a sterile husband allowing his wife to visit a neighbour to get pregnant. Every small community had a 'fils du cure'. Then there are the complications of religion, class, the generational divide between Parisians and provincials, city dwellers and villagers but throughout all that sex is just matter of fact, we are pretty honest about love and lust, there's nothing sordid about the latter; that's what I feel for you, just pure lust and I understand completely if you don't love me or see love in me. Or even want to suck my big toe, and you know that really turns me on! 'To be frank Sylvie, you are a two-man job!' said Pascal.

Sylvie laughed then added 'I don't need to be stroked or petted, neither do I crave affection or constant attention. Men and women should be free to act as they please despite any peculiar fixations! No one can regulate the affairs between men and women, unless it needs to be anyone else's business, it's nobody's business.'

Pascal thought how well educated and spoken Sylvie was, a natural woman of the world, the modern world.

They mulled the conversation over, had another swig of cognac each and decided to put the thoughts away for the night. The bombing went on relentless

Thirty-Seven

DIFFICULT QUESTIONS

MAY 18, 1944

After supper that evening Yvette decided to challenge Wolfie about Poland and Germany.

'Wolfie' she said, 'when French people get sent to Germany to work, are they treated well? Do they get enough food to eat?'

'Aha, you have been listening to terrorist gossip. This is the department of home security, the SD and as far as I know they are treated correctly.

'I hear some of them look like skin and bone,' said Yvette. 'I heard this from someone who had been a soldier in 1940 and was released and returned home in exchange for ten more workers being sent,' Said Yvette

'Yes, we do have exchange programmes for genuine prisoners, but I honestly don't know how they are treated' said Wolfie with a big disarming smile. Yvette's heart melted slightly but much as she loved him, she pressed on.

"and what about Poland? They say if you get sent there you will never come back,' Said Yvette.

The disarming smile had vanished.

'Look my little Yvette, I wasn't ever in Poland so I can't say what happened there. I know there were prison camps, and many Jews were shipped there to work. I was sent straight to Russia in 1943. By then we only had 2,000 soldiers left out of 15,000 in our division and we refitted down here outside Bordeaux. I joined them for a great tank battle at Kursk. But we were already on the retreat. Some bad things happened in Russia on our side and the Russians. It was just total war with no quarter given and I was fortunate to get out alive and be shipped down here out of a freezing hell to recuperate. We were the fighting side of the SS, the Waffen SS. We didn't concern ourselves with the political side. We just focussed every day on staying alive. I am a soldier and respect my enemy. I am not a sadistic killer.'

Yvette was quiet. Maybe Wolfie was telling the truth.

Claude and Jenny were exhausted. They had been training more young boys desperate to escape the STO and who thought that life in the woods would be a life of ease without any danger. Claude disillusioned them by showing pictures of fighting and demonstrating field craft and weapon handling. Claude noticed that in another four or five days the moon was going to start waxing again and then there would be a very full moon in June. This made him tingle because he knew that the invasion conditions could only get better from now on.

General Lammerding and his general staff were busy trying to chase up supplies of ammunition and general stores they had ordered. Spare parts for the tanks were the main problem. Everything was being shipped to the Eastern front which was consuming vast amounts of material. Knowing the conditions there and the rate of attrition he was surprised that the factories were still managing to work in view of the huge air raids now plastering all the German cities. But the morale of his army was paramount. He had investigated getting minor parts made locally but there was always the problem of sabotage. He called a conference of senior officers to brief them on the latest intelligence reports.

'Gentlemen, the Abwehr has reported large build-up of forces in SE England. The theory is that they will attack the Pas de Calais although a feinting and diversionary attack may come in the Dieppe area'. Personally, I wouldn't do that if I was Eisenhower. I would come west to Normandy where there are better beaches and not so many SS divisions waiting. But our spies are hard at work in England, and I will from now on receive daily Abwehr reports. The options of the Allies attacking through the South of France have been largely discounted due to the long logistic lines necessary for that. In the meantime, my order of the day is to ban all civilian rail traffic between Montauban and Poitiers. We now need that line exclusively for military traffic and we have lost a lot of rolling stock and locomotives which we will need if we have to move north.'

MAY 19, 1944

Back in England, Buckmaster was concerned at the

penetration of his circuits in France. Since 1941 he had sent over 450 agents to France, 39 of them being women and had lost 10 of the female agents due to betrayals. But he persisted with female agents because they were able to blend in better than men. Some were just careless operators; however, he was worried about reports reaching him from the Correze and the Dordogne just from routine sweeps and searches: in the `Correze 250 maquis and civilians had been killed and 190 deported; in Dordogne over 700 killed and 300 deported- and the *Das Reich* hadn't even started on their journey north; these were insurrections being put down by forward elements of the *Das Reich*.

Claude had heard rumours about these actions but hardly believed them to be true. What would the point be? It would only stiffen resistance and waste time for such a frontline fighting force. But he got Jenny to send the rumours through over the wire. She got an answer back straightway requesting more information about *Das Reich*

So, Claude and Jenny decided to walk into Montauban and check out the situation. Train activity was not as much as usual but in the Café over an even more dreadful coffee and a soul saving cognac, they learned that civilian trains had been cut by 95% to make space for military traffic. So that was one clue that things were different. And there was an even larger number of German soldiers about, different units of *Das Reich*. Claude made a mental note of the flashes on their shoulders. There were at least three new regiments.

3rd SS Panzergrenadier Regiment "Deutschland"
4th SS Panzergrenadier Regiment "Der Fuhrer"

And 2nd SS Panzer Regiment

'C'mon' said Claude quietly; it's getting rather too hot for comfort in here. In truth the temperature on this beautiful day was already in excess of 30c and likely to reach 33c by midday, but it was the excess of field grey and black uniforms that were unnerving him and making him hotter.

'Let's take a stroll be the river.' Claude was wearing his peasant uniform today, no bow tie and hat. He felt that had outlived its shelf life here in Montauban.

They walked slowly hand in hand to the embankment where the river Tarn rushed over the weir and settled down into languid pools of slow-moving water as it drifted under the magnificent roman bridge. They joined the throngs of young French people doing the same thing; staring at the waters still full of ice melt as it travelled down to Bordeaux and the sea.

Claude had never asked Jenny about her background, for security reasons but decided a few questions wouldn't go amiss.

'tell me about your upbringing, the real upbringing' he said speaking in French.

Jenny was quiet for a moment then said 'my parents were very straightlaced middle class and I went to an all-girls boarding school in Henley when I was nine years old; daddy was in the RAF and just been posted abroad at that time; so, I was sent away. My elder sister stayed home with mum and my younger brother in our house in Theale. They thought I needed the routine and structure of a boarding school to help combat my asthma at the time and it did so by the age of 19 I was fairly clear of it. I avoided the cross country running though, especially the early morning runs because the cold air made my chest tight. Although it was a very traditional blue stockinged school with plenty of netball and jolly old hockey sticks to toughen one up, the matron there was very kind and took pity on me because in those days, asthma was a bit of a rarity, and I was the only girl in school who suffered from it; so, I was regarded as a bit of a leper really! While they were all out running, I used to dream and make up poems in my head where-ever I was. I used to love stories about Bears, in fact Madam la Grange told me the other day that there are still plenty of brown bears in the Pyrenees.' Jenny looked south to the mountain range in the distance; a blue hazy line of hills folded over one another until the peaks rising up tall were still covered in snow could be seen in the distance.

'And I guess somewhere there are RAF pilots who have been shot down now trying to cross those very brown bear mountains into neutral Spain, trying to get back to England, only to be put back into circulation again. I would like to go back, I don't have a good feeling about this mission Claude, we haven't moved around enough, and our luck will run out.'

Claude said 'tell me a poem then, about where we are now"

Jenny laughed. 'No, go on, anything silly, short and sweet will do' said Claude smiling.

'well, because I miss home and old father Thames with its banks of weeping willows right down to waters' edge, here are my thoughts right now; she lent close and whispered in his ear in English.

'Take me to where the weeping willow grows
On the banks of the river where lazy waters flow.
There in the valley of the bears I could end my ways,
With buttercups and butterflies to help my passing days'

Claude kissed her on the cheek, smiled and said 'so sweet. Mixing old father Thames with the Pyrenees and bears. We must move on; we have tarried too long!' They walked back through the town and were amazed at the amount of information they could pick up just from the uniforms and activity which Jenny could send off tonight to Buckmaster.

Thirty-Eight

NEWS OF PASCAL

MAY 22ND 1944 FULL MOON 100% GEMINI

Yvette was full of hope that the new moon would bring her good luck; she was a Gemini and as the Moon in Gemini manifests itself by the need for changes and spontaneity, she was feeling it's about time change happened. She was thinking about her feelings and sharing them with others. She could, she thought be more talkative and speak with others more easily these days but when it came to it, she found it difficult. One might have a better ability to keep a cool head, but always beware, cold heart can discourage others. Harmony of thinking and feeling is important. Harmony with Yves was not good; he had become quite bossy recently and Mama was even mor introspective than usual, worried about food; where was the next meal going to come from. Inwardly she was very pleased with the rabbits Yves brought her and of course with the bread from next door. It was very warm weather again. Mama was worried about Yvette who seemed to have withdrawn from her, no longer confiding secrets and worries like she used to. Whatever was afoot, Yvette wasn't sharing her feelings with anyone.

Yvette often wondered what had happened to Pascal. She no longer cried herself to sleep, just had a lost yearning for something she once knew; it was called the future, a husband, a home, and babies. And that future had drained away. Sure, she had Wolfie; fortunately, he had taken over her life but where was Pascal.

That evening at supper, Wolfie came in again with Wilhelm; they were laughing and joking. Wolfie went straight to the piano and started to play a tune Yvette had never heard before – it was a German marching song *'Panzerleid"* dedicated to their tanks. Wilhelm put his arm around Wolfie and said 'you know Wolfie, when our division went into Russia, it was part of the biggest German campaign ever; nearly 4 million soldiers, 4,000 tanks, 3,000 half-tracks, 20,000 artillery pieces, over 600,000 vehicles, and the horses, yes the poor old horses. And in those days, we had the Luftwaffe, over 3,000 planes; now we have none. They are nowhere to be seen.' Wilhelm paused and drank another glass of wine. Yves was drumming on the tabletop with the kitchen knives. The men were both more than now slightly drunk singing at the top of their voices, and good voices they were, Wilhelm's was deep and very melodious. When they stopped the marching song, they went straight into *'Lili Marl*ene' with Wolfie playing the high notes precisely and in time; halfway through they lapsed into English. And when they stopped again Yvette managed to butt in and say 'boys, you have had too much to drink! Supper is ready, come and sit down'. She felt as though these were her big strong brothers who would protect her.

Yves wanted to know why they sang some verses of a German song in English.

'It's an international song, it was very popular with our great general Rommel in the Africa Korps, and we know the Tommies liked it as well. When I was on the eastern front it was played every night by radio Belgrade at 10pm; and it was a great drinking song.

'Yes, but what was it about' repeated Yves

'It was about a soldier on duty in his sentry box and every night he watched a girl, a nurse, going off duty and she always smiled and waved at him'.

'Is that all?' laughed Yves?

'Well young man, when you are a lonely soldier and missing your girlfriend it's always nice to be waved at by a pretty girl, you think of her as your own girl'.

Yves said, 'tell me about your Tank – is it the best?' Both laughed, but of course said Wilhelm. It's not a Tiger but a Panther 5, somewhat more reliable than a Tiger and faster. And with the new 75mm Kwk42L70 gun it can penetrate anything!

'Poof' said Yves, throwing his arms up wide.

'And Wilhelm, how did you get into the SS? 'Ah well my father was postmaster with a village store during world War 1 but after Germany lost the war, everything was taken, and our family had to sell everything just for food. Me, because I came from a poor non-military family, I was rejected by the army, but the SS took me and made me feel proud again. I was very good at sport and in good health with no injuries, not even a bad tooth or filling, the SS would never have taken me with dental problems. So, I owe everything to the SS'

'And what about Russia. Is it a scary wild and terrible place?' asked Yves. Wolfie replied 'Its huge, vast, and the Russians weren't scary, they were good but brutal fighters and we respected them. The big enemy was the cold; the cold killed the horses, it killed the men, it killed the machinery. Frostbite in ten seconds unless covered up, boots overwrapped with straw'

Wilhelm, 'don't you get scared of death?' asked Yves

'You have a lot of questions! 'said Wolfie

'We are young men, 22 years old, we are never going to die!' replied Wilhelm

'Ah my little Yvette, you are my *Lili Marlene'* said Wolfie, 'I forgot, I have some good news for you!' He hoisted her onto his lap.

"I received a report from the Gestapo about your boyfriend'. Yvette sat bolt upright. 'Yes, said Wolfie, the car taking him to the train was ambushed just outside Poitiers by a British Spitfire. It shot up the car and all the occupants, that's the bad news but the good news is that your friend was not amongst the dead. All the other passengers were identified, eventually -because the car burnt badly'

'So said Yvette. Where is he?'

'That we don't know; maybe he escaped into the hills and is in hiding somewhere.

A rush of blood coursed through Yvette's veins and her heart thundered so loud she was sure the whole room could hear it. Maybe Pascal was alive.

'You will have to wait for someone to be in touch, news will come one way or the other. If he has been recaptured by the Germans that will be easy for me to find out but if the Milice, French police or the maquis have caught him we can't do anything about that. Your best bet is to contact your local resistance movement and ask them' said Wolfie giving her a pinch on the cheek.

'It's time for us to go to bed' said Wilhelm, 'one more drink for our Panzer Kameraden', and a double schnapps each got them laughing and joking again. Wolfie stood up very erect and hauled Wilhelm to his feet. 'Say goodnight, Willy' he said. Wilhelm stood erect and smiled at the family, a big beaming smile from his lean reedy frame, and strong sculptured ayrian face and thanked mama Yvette and Yves in turn for a splendid evening. They both kissed mama and Yvette on the cheeks, Wilhelm left and Wolfie went to his room.

Mama and Yvette cleared up. 'You know Yvette' said Mama, they are both such lovely boys, pity they are Germans and the enemy; wearing a French uniform and either of them would make wonderful husbands; courteous, handsome, virile, and charming. What a difference being born into a different culture makes you. Just the throw of the dice or the way the cards a dealt.'

'I have a handsome courteous boyfriend Mama,' said Yvette. You remember Pascal, don't you?'

'Aha, Pascal, but who knows where he is and if he will ever return; he may be dead or in Poland in one of those camps' said mama. At this Yvette burst into tears. This surprised Mama because Yvette was not normally so sensitive. Was there something wrong with her she thought. Maybe she ought to see the doctor just in case. But she dropped the idea and after Yvette had calmed down, they kissed goodnight with several sloppy bisous and went to bed.

MAY 23RD

Yvette asked Yves to go to the café and see if Terri was there. He scampered off happy to see his country tutor who was the love of his life although he would never admit to that. But Terri was a great friend and a real tomboy who was teaching Yves about life. Sure enough, Terri was sitting there drinking a glass of red wine and chatting to a girlfriend.

Hi Yves, what's up she said? "My sister Yvette wants to see you, can you come to the house?"

'Ah, said Terri, "we are having a philosophical discussion about men; you see Yves we need our men back but, in the meantime does one fraternise with the enemy just to feel the lovely soft skin on their blonde hulky bodies once more or does one stay celibate and wait for our boys to come back from Germany or the resistance, if ever if either.? The trouble is you can't get that close to those sodden soldiers to smell them, if I like the way they walk and smile then I still have to smell that man scent and bury my nose in his hair!'

Terri's friend Michelle, who Yves had never seen before, piped up and said, 'I keep telling Terri that we can endlessly philosophise and that is a fool's errand because there is more philosophy in this bottle of red wine than in all the books on philosophy, so live for the moment I say!

If these soldiers want to visit the brothels in Toulouse to have French girls, they can have this one (me) right now instead– and I won't even charge them! There's no such thing as infidelity, that suggests you weren't faithful with your body; but your body belongs to you, not to anyone else – that's philosophical sharing and communal crap!'

'Michelle, calm down, You are frustrated, tipsy and sex mad like une *chienne en chaleur*"

said Terri. They both laughed. Michelle retorted with a giggle 'I am not a salope en chaleur! Don't be so rude to me. 'C'mon Yves, this is girls talk, let's go see your sister,' said Terri.

Michelle tweaked Yves on the cheek and smiled 'any time you want to meet my pretty little sister, let me know!' Yves blushed.

They walked to the house where Yvette welcomed them in, and they sat around the piano. Yvette was playing Bach again. 'What's up? asked Terri.

Yvette told her that she had had news of Pascal and wondered if the resistance could trace him. He was last seen in the vicinity east of Limoges having escaped from the Germans. 'Well, it's a huge area that *Parc naturel regional des Millevaches* en Limousin, lots of rolling hills, forests and lakes. I hear the Germans don't even patrol there anymore because the maquis own it and travel unhindered around it. So, he could be anywhere; if he is still alive,' said Terri. Yvette flinched but didn't respond. "I will put the word out,' said Terri

Thirty-Nine

YOU HAVE TO DREAM

Claude and Jenny were logging all the vehicles passing down the route National from a vantage point high in the woods. With every day that passed, Claude was more and more anxious that their luck would not hold out. Jenny was becoming paranoid with every German she saw and feared that any day they would be caught and shot or put on a freight train going east. How could it be that after four years of war the Germans still had so many men and lorries. She had no idea that Germany was running its factories on slave labour. French workers deported to Germany to work just ended up as slaves, dying where they worked.

'Claude' have you any idea how many French are now in the resistance movement? Would it be enough to help us if we got into trouble down here?'

'No, it wouldn't be enough, we are on our own. We have each other and that's it. The last assessment I got from Baker street was that there are less than 1% of French people in the resistance and fewer than that in the active maquis. Maybe that will change when the allies come. But for the moment France is passive. The most we can hope for is that the landings come soon; that will cause chaos and we will be more hidden with chaos. Chaos will help us. And the last intelligence I had before we left was that Germany has over 310 divisions in the field, an insane number of men under arms, ten times what they had in 1940 when they invaded France. However, the Luftwaffe is a spent force and the Kreigsmarine virtually defeated so we only have the German army to worry about, I am sure the Russians are hammering the Wehrmacht in the east!'

How can that be' said Jenny, if they have taken the luxury of shipping one of their finest divisions from the eastern front down here to a quiet sector?' She spoke. 'Things can't be all that good for the Russians'

Claude was silent. Jenny had a point. 'Then Claude said, Look, I know it's tough, don't you think I am questioning why we are here, what we are doing seems pointless. Counting this and counting that. We just must believe in something, think of something to hang onto, a childhood memory, your favoured cinema or dance hall, we can do this together, pick a subject and every day we will tell each other our memories. Jenny, you have to dream, you must be strong, you have to think that you will win and get home alive. They won't pull us out now, we are here for a purpose, the fact that the *Das Reich* has been pulled out of the east and sent here means they know something we don't. And they know that because we are still alive that we have found a way of surviving. That we have a system, an organisation, a method, and we have luck on our side, so don't be paranoid. It's just a different uniform that you see, they are all human beings and I know war makes animals out of human beings but hold your head up high and keep your spirits up. We just have to keep counting and training the French maquis. There are dozens of young French men in the hills, most just hiding but some are brave enough to be trainable for fighting'

MAY 25TH

Yves came home with a message for Yvette from Terri, asking her to come to the farmhouse tomorrow. The next day both Yves and Yvette walked casually to the farm and were met by the usual cacophony of barking dogs, chickens clucking and the one and only snorting pig left. They were welcomed inside and offered lemonade made with fresh lemons. Terri told Yves to go out and collect some eggs and came to the point.

'We have three British fliers hiding in the barn. They will be leaving tonight, the passeurs will take them to a village high up in the Pyrenees where they will spend the night and cross over to Spain the next night'

'Stop there' said Yvette, 'why are you telling me this? We could be shot just for knowing they are here. It's stupid, what has it got to do with us?'

'Well said Terri, I just thought your German boyfriend could intercede on our behalf if things go wrong, after all he is probably the cause of that bump in your tummy'.

'Yvette was shocked; 'first there is no bump and if there was a bump then that would be due to Pascal before he went away and second the so- called German boyfriend is a soldier and could never intercede on your behalf; that is such a stupid ignorant belief, the crassest idea I have ever heard. All soldiers have a job to do, and I would never be able to stop them or interfere. Forget it Terri' she said scowling. 'Why are you getting involved with these airmen? If they are captured, they will just go to a prisoner of war camp and sit out the war; you and us and our families will go to the camp of no return if they don't shoot us first.

'Well, 'said Terri. 'It's not just fliers that pass down this *chemin de la liberte*, French and Dutch people on the run, Jews and English spies also use our route. In fact, I have a cousin called Albert, about my age who lives in Castelnou, One of the villages high up on the French side in the Pyrenees. I haven't seen him for four years, but before the war started, I went on holiday to his farm; he was only 15 then but already well into his training to be a shepherd, I can remember how he dressed, in his woollen brown smock and heavy overcoat for the cold mountain nights, dark blue serge trousers, big, nailed boots, his leather satchel, black beret at a cocky angle and shepherd crook; I had quite a crush on him then. He looked so proud of being entrusted with the village flock. I would love to be with him today as right now he will be high up on the summer pastures, in a mountain hut just a stone throw from the Spanish border. He will be with his sheepdogs, his two faithful dogs and a donkey: just the sound of the sheep with their tinkling bells, the lambs bleating and the donkey braying and at night all the stars a twinkling tapestry for his ceiling. I stayed in the hut with him for a few nights, we laughed and joked about who we were going to marry, he had his eyes on a village girl and was going to build her a big house on the mountain by the stream – I would love to know if he did.'

'Why does he have a donkey with him" asked Yvette, suddenly entranced at this romantic story.

'He milks the ewes, makes lovely cheese and every week loads the donkey up with the cheese and takes it down to the village and returns the same night with stores and provisions. He leaves the dogs in charge; in case an eagle tries to pick off a lamb; and there are wolves up there as well so one dog would help the other if a wolf came'

'How long does he stay up there" asked Yvette.

'The whole summer, about three months.'

"wow 'said Yvette, 'That's a long time.'

'Yes, but it's so beautiful up there, just nature all around you, the smell of the sheep and the grass, the sight of an eagle soaring high in the sky, the running mountain streams so crystal clear you can drink from them and provided you don't get ill or attacked by a brown Bear then its idyllic; I sometimes wish I could be there, like now to get away from all the Germans'

'Attacked by a bear, are there really bears up there?' asked Yvette 'I've never seen a bear"

"You don't want to meet one, with one swipe of his paw a big male bear could knock a dogs head off. but apart from the fliers, my cousin gives refuge in his hut to all the others I mentioned'

'But surely that is so dangerous with all the German patrols, don't they catch people?

Yes, from time to time they do but that's mainly because the passeurs have been betrayed by French people keen to earn a reward from the Germans. Otherwise, they know the mountains like the back of their hands, there are many trails and passes across and they know how to avoid the patrols. It's dangerous in winter, they don't cross then with the little Jewish children and anyway the tracks in the snow can easily be followed.'

Suddenly Yvette was overcome with pride at being associated with Terri and the 'freedom trail', she wished she was as brave as Terri. Yves interrupted her thoughts saying he had collected six eggs and was proudly carrying them wrapped in paper in a sack.

On the way home Yvette realised why Terri had told her all this; it was to enmesh her further into Terri's world of resistance, she was getting deeper and deeper involved without knowing it. Her mind was in turmoil. Here was Wolfie the enemy helping to find Pascal and there was Terri her friend wanting to kill the enemy. She was worried about her tummy; she suspected she might be pregnant, and Mama had noticed how off colour she was and that she should see the doctor. Maybe she would see him tomorrow.

Forty

BETRAYED

MAY 26

It was just after dawn that Pascal heard engines approaching their hideout, then men speaking in German. The day before they had finished distributing the medicines and medical supplies stolen from the store a few nights before. Everybody who received them were extremely grateful, even for a small packet of aspirins. Some wanted more and Pascal thought how there were good men who had died to obtain what they had.

Sylvie, Pascal, and the others leapt to get their backpacks together and then grabbed their weapons. Just then, their lookout Hugo came crashing in shouting 'les boches!'

'Leave everything, run, Disperse and meet at the old cave in the woods' shouted Sylvie. As they ran out the back entrance they heard shots, and the sound of dogs barking. Pascal and Sylvie ran together then separated. Pascal did not head north up the hill to the old cave.

Instead, he ran south towards the river, now hardly more than a stream in the summer heat. He ploughed into the cool water and splashed his way for fifty metres or so until he came to a thick copse, that came down to the water's edge. He was more afraid of the dogs than the Germans and hopefully they would have lost the scent in the water. He worked his way quietly through the woods and then spotted a farmhouse. He was just about to go to it when he heard raised voices, speaking German 'If you see any of these saboteurs you must report it. We will leave two soldiers here to protect you' the German officer in charge said. Then the remaining six men got in the half track and left. Pascal sat down and opened his backpack. He had 2 apples, half a large sausage, three grenades, two full clips for the Sten-gun a few bullets for the pistol stuck in his belt and a bottle of water. Hardly enough to start a war with. Then he heard rapid gunfire coming from the north, the direction of the cave. He ate an apple, drank half the water and thought desperately about his options. He was surprised at the speed and extent of the cordon the Germans had thrown around the whole area. Nearby there was an axe stuck in a tree trunk left no doubt by the woodcutter. It gave him and idea. There was no way he had enough ammunition, or the desire to try and fight his way out so using his knife he dug a hole by the tree, stripped the Sten down to eleven smaller parts, placing it and the grenades into the soft sandy earth, covered it up, rubbed some dirt into his face to and hands, then took the axe from the tree trunk, slung it over his shoulder and walked towards the farmhouse. The two soldiers on guard there unslung their rifles and challenged him. Although he could perfectly understand what they were saying, he addressed them in French and laid on a thick guttural accent which he hoped would convince them that he was a local peasant. They responded in very broken French mixed with German. They were very young, maybe 17 or 18 only. Their uniforms seemed too big for them, and the coalscuttle helmets completely dwarfed their heads. Pascal realised that his identity papers were very rudimentary forgeries but maybe he could bluff his way past them into open country. He asked them where they were from, but they did not understand so he asked them again in German. The lanky one replied 'Stuttgart' and the smaller one 'Hanover', then the lanky one asked 'are you German?'

'No French but I come from Alsace Lorraine, so I am bilingual,' said Pascal. 'Ah, I have relatives in Kolmar' said the lanky one. 'But sadly, I have not seen them for five years. It's a lovely town in upper Alsace.' 'Yes, I know it well, lied Pascal. They chatted while the small one examined his papers, pointing out that his travel document was out of date, and he must get it renewed. Other than that, it seemed the papers were alright. They asked him what he had been doing in the woods, but Pascal managed to persuade them that he had been clearing the trees to make way for the farmers pigs. And why wasn't he in the German army? Pascal said he had French nationality and was in the French army at the start of the war but had lost his army papers during the bombing. His identity card stated he was French. Pascal switched the conversation to the sound of gunfire earlier to which the small one said 'We were rooting out some terrorists from the woods who had robbed our medicine store and killed our men, we were pulled off duty of guarding the rail yards at Poitiers where there has been devastation night after night from the British. Pascal kept up the conversation asking them about their families while all the time looking in the distance trying to recognise a farmhouse he knew. He saw one and at a natural break in the conversation he said pointing to the distant farmhouse 'well, nice to meet you, now I must go to my home over there and do some more work'.

The two young soldiers acknowledged his departure and he walked off slowly, axe over the shoulder in true woodcutter's style.

Forty-One

A LITTLE BABY BOY
FOR FRANCE

MAY 27

Yvette sat in front of Doctor Bernard Caviller, who had been the family doctor for decades. He was almost retired now being in his late sixties but still came to the surgery in a suit and tie. He had delivered Yvette and Yves, treated their father for bad flu one winter and of course helped her mother during her pregnancy. He sat as usual in his little surgery, one desk, one chair, a screen and a lie flat bed, and some boxes with medical apparatus. 'Hello, my little Yvette, what brings you here? You don't look very well at all. 'I have been sick this morning she said, and yesterday and the day before. It won't go away". She was trembling and sweating. At 8am the day was already very warm. He took her pulse and temperature, looked at her tongue and then asked her when she had her last period. She told him. He gently examined her breasts and said 'my dear mademoiselle, you are sick because there is no doubt that you are pregnant, and a little French baby is on the way! Who is the father?

Yvette thought hard but was surprised how she lied so easily, 'it's Pascal, the farmer but he has been taken away.' 'The STO asked the doctor?' 'No, the gestapo, he is an Alsatian and they wanted to force him to join the German army; they just took him away and I have heard nothing from him'

'That's unusual' said Bernard' the Germans are always punctilious about letting their French captors send back a lovely postcard full of propaganda about how great life is in the Wehrmacht and how well fed they are. Maybe it's just got lost in the post. Now, don't worry yourself, you must eat properly, you have a little life to feed".

Dr Bernard had seen many things in his life, having survived The Great War as he called it. He was too old to be a combatant but had been in the medical corps at Verdun. There was nothing he didn't know about pain and horror. In between the wars he had grown very fond of all things English, especially the language, the etiquette, history, and the Royal Family. He had met the English soldiers at Verdun and struck up an acquaintance with a captain of artillery who he had kept in touch with until 1940.

Yvette left the surgery all mixed up in her mind; she had betrayed Pascal, her father would be mad, certainly upset and Wolfie, how was she going to tell him that his baby was going to be born in France, as a French baby. And then all her friends, how was she going to tell them that she had a baby with Wolfgang of the hated German enemy? She wanted to talk to someone and ironically it was Terri she sought out. She went straight to the farm and openly told Terri about the pregnancy. She had tears in her eyes as she burbled out the whole story and almost wailed when she asked what was she going to do? Terri was very pragmatic; 'first you don't tell anyone, this is a wonderful natural event and hopefully it will be a little boy to help replace all our lost sons; second, who knows what will happen to either Pascal or Wolfie; they may both never return. My odds are on Pascal coming back and Wolfie being killed or captured when the *Das Reich* comes up against the Americans as surely, they will.

'How can you say such Terrible things, you can't talk about them that way; they are both human beings and enthroned in my life one way or another!' Yvette almost yelled the words out.

Calm down, let's look at the facts; when did you last have sex with Pascal?

'I never did,' shouted Yvette.!

'Alright, what was the date you had your wild silly escapade with Wolfgang?' Asked Terri.

Yvette told her and Terri, putting her hand on Yvette's said, and just before that, Pascal was taken away. So, it could easily have been him n'est-ce pas?

Yvette could see the logic of what Terri was saying. But it wasn't true.

'So, you must brave it out, lie your head off until the time comes. Many people are lying their way out of trouble every day just to survive. This war will end this year, that's what all the maquis are saying. As soon as the allies land, the whole population of the southwest will rise up and kick the German's and their whores out of here and then we will execute all the French Milice and their traitor bosses in Vichy, much blood will flow!

Yvette was quiet now. Terri had found her a way out for her. She kissed and hugged Terri who was a bit taken aback by the warmth but appreciated the gesture.

'What about Mama?' asked Yvette. 'Alors, you have to tell her that Pascal gave you a "going away present" a few hours before he was taken. Really, I don't know what you should tell your mother, but it doesn't really matter. Don't make up excuses, just tell the truth that you are pregnant and proud of having a baby with Pascal. The timing is great, nine months from now and there will be no war. Yvette felt calm and comforted but was still troubled about her joint betrayal; however, time was on her side and now her own little war was internal, how to make sure this crumb of a life inside her was going to survive and that it was up to her alone to make sure it survived.

Forty-Two

INTO THE FIRE

nside the signal box Raoul was cursing the hot weather. It was very small place for him to work in and the signal levers were getting hot to handle. There was news of more low loader wagons coming which needed to find space in the already overcrowded sidings. This could only mean one thing; the *Das Reich* is getting ready to move. He asked Hans if he knew anything, 'ach nein, everybody is now on alert but that doesn't mean anything, every other day is an alert. There are rumours of course, but I don't know anything else. All I know is there are more manoeuvres every day, it seems General Lammerding wants to wear his men out before they even get to grips with the allies, but on the other hand there are a lot of replacements coming in, younger and younger it seems to me. Just boys. So, something is in the wind. We are expecting more tanks tomorrow, the new Panther mark V, about 60 to add to the 64-mark fours we have scattered around the town. So maybe the general staff expect the allies to come across from Africa and land in the south of France around Marseilles.'

'That doesn't make sense, 'said Raoul, 'they would be a long way from their supply lines, and they are not going to strip out any forces from Italy; they are all tied up there in knots courtesy of your General Kesselring no, it makes more sense to invade in the Bordeaux area, but that doesn't make sense either when again you consider the supply lines. The big question is that if they invade in the North, say in Normandy, what is a crack SS Division doing down here? It can't be just to wipe out the maquis. That would be a futile waste of such strength. Maybe the low loaders will be going North.'

Ironically, this same conversation was being conducted by General Lammerding with his chief of staff Willy Froam, they had no information from OKW except that von Rundstedt had demanded the end to the maquis attacks on isolated German outposts. The maquis were getting very bold and roaming at will. Even the civilian population was getting fed up with them because they looted food, destroyed property and murdered Vichy officials.

MAY 28, 1944

Pascal arrived at the farmhouse about a kilometer from where he had chatted to the two young German soldiers. He was still carrying his axe in woodcutter mode. A young girl opened the door and said her mother was not at home. Pascal asked if he could have a glass of water. She looked doubtful but finally went back inside and brought out an earthenware jug of water which Pascal gratefully drew deep slugs from and poured the final amount over his head cooling everything down in the hot midday sun. She stared at him. 'Where is your father?' he asked. She didn't answer. Pascal could feel something wasn't right, so he decided to move on south and find somewhere else. He thanked the girl and walked out over the uplands into a hamlet. It was market day, but it was a pitiful market; stands were empty of fruit, vegetables, no ducks' geese, or chickens, just a few languid hares and rabbits strung up with flies already settling into them. There were only two very haggard old ladies in the street trying to sell some chairs. They looked at Pascal curiously. He wondered if he should speak to them at all, opening a conversation could be dangerous. But he was hungry, so he approached them and asked 'Excuse me but do you have a piece of bread please? Both ladies looked quizzically at him and said in a quiet voice 'non monsieur désolé. They then motioned to the other end of the village putting their fingers to their lips. Pascal sensed danger and turned around and walked back the way he came. Whatever was going on there he didn't want to be a part of it.

Then he could hear gunfire from the other end of the village, a single machine gun then several single shots.

He walked quickly back down the field to the farmhouse and decided to try again. This time an old man bent double came to the door and asked who he was and what did he want. Pascal told him he was a woodcutter and needed some bread. The old man said, 'come in, but you can't stay." They both went inside to the darkened kitchen. There the little girl was playing with a well-worn rosette, clearly not hers. The old man pulled out a very thin baguette and tore off a piece, Pascal said thank you and slowly chewed the bread. The rest of the baguette was wrapped in a damp cloth and put away. 'Désolé monsieur but that is all we have left for tonight.'

"Where is everyone?" asked Pascal. The old man sat down, and tears were in his eyes. "The gendarmes came and questioned everyone here and in the hamlet about the gang that looted a pharmacy and shot four Germans and three gendarmes the other night. They have taken her mother and father away, as hostages. I don't know how I can look after her. We have nothing to eat in the house and I can't manage the walk to the village.'

"I think the village is under German control' said 'Pascal. I have just come from there and its virtually deserted and there's gunfire. I suspect they are shooting hostages." The little girl ran closer to the old man and hugged him; Pascal presumed him to be her grandfather.

Clearly, he should not stay here a moment longer; but he was trapped. He desperately wanted to help them but how? He only had a small amount of money and his axe. At least he could chop wood for a fire and make the kitchen more cheerful. The little girl had gone into the pantry and suddenly came out with three potatoes and a big smile on her face. That was a start. Maybe Pascal could make some potato soup and add some herbs from the garden. They got to work and soon were sitting down with three bowls of soup and the rest of the baguette.

The reality of the maquis activity in trying to do something good in stealing medicines for the needy had gone badly wrong. Pascal felt guilty at having wreaked havoc on a small community and he knew the arithmetic, for every German killed, there would be eleven innocent civilians shot or deported. That would make 77 murders. He sighed and wondered had it been worth it.

He decided the best thing to do was to retrace his steps and somehow find Sylvie; she would know what to do. He told grandpa and the girl that he was going to get help and set out into the dusky evening. He got to the place where he had found the axe and replaced it in the same block of tree trunk. Then traversed the stream towards where he and the others had exited the camp. There was no one there. Maybe he should go to the cave where Sylvie said she was going. By the time he got there it was dark and no one to be seen. He was so tired that he swayed on his feet; he needed to rest and took the opportunity to sleep on the bracken outside.

He was woken by a kick in the ribs and a torch shining in his face. A gruff French voice shouted in his face. Two French Gendarmes were pointing their guns at him and motioned him to move to a truck. Wearily and stiffly, he moved slowly and got in the truck. They then drove him to the French detention centre, south of Poitiers on the Route de Limoges. It was a simple barbed wire compound full of gypsies and Romanies, a transit camp en route to somewhere worse. The truck stopped at the makeshift office, and he was shoved inside. The French Milice Inspector was curt, demanding what he was doing in the woods. Pascal decided to tell the truth but shortened the time scale of the car being strafed to yesterday and that today he was sleeping after escaping the wreckage. The inspector believed him but concluded that he would have to hand him over to the Gestapo. Pascal pleaded with him, to no avail, but as a concession the Inspector said he would move him today to Poitier – 'this transit camp is not for you' he said. 'We have to supply our quota of Jews daily to the Germans 'but in order to help save as many French Jews as possible, we tell them we have no Jews today and offer them gypsies and Romanies instead. The Germans are keen to clean up all undesirables from their Reich so this lot are bound for a three day one way journey to a holiday camp in eastern Poland tomorrow" he said pointing to the cattle cars in the siding.

Forty-Three

THE NEWS IS OUT

MAY 29TH 1944

Yvette returned home from the doctors and as soon as she entered the house, mama said 'so what did the doctor say? Have you got something wrong with you?'

Yvette took a deep breath and said 'mama, you are going to be a grandmother'

Mama gasped and asked quietly and menacingly 'who is the father?'

Yvette replied quickly 'Pascal'

'Well, that's the good news as it would have been terrible if the father was a German, the shame that would bring on this family, however the bad news is that Pascal is nowhere to be seen so who is going to bring up this baby, and what on? Thin air?

"I am going to bring it up' retorted Yvette, suddenly angry at her mother's aggressive tone 'and a few days ago you were saying what fine young men our German lodgers are"

'Yes, but they are still Germans and the enemy of our country, what would your father say if he heard you talking like this?'

"I am so sad mama that you are so judgemental and not happy to be a grandmother. I hate you!' and with that Yvette slammed the door and went to her room tears streaming down her face.

Mama went next door to talk to Madelaine and told her the news. Madelaine listened and said, 'don't be too harsh on your daughter. Listen to her. Understand the circumstances and be supportive. I feel very confident that Pascal will return. He is a survivor and if there is one bit of good news to come out of this dreadful period then the advent of a new life is to be cherished. God knows we have lost so many lives anyway and we need to rebuild our nation and our families. By the time the baby is born I am sure France will be free of the Germans. The Allies will come. maybe next month. They have to come in the summer so let me help you and Yvette to prepare. There is much to be done in the next few months'

Francoise touched her arm and said 'thank you for your support. I feel better now. I will talk to Yvette this evening.

But the planned heart to heart between mother and daughter didn't have time to materialise. In came Wolfie and Wilhelm, both of them bringing food and in a happy cheerful mood. Wolfie had a bag of sausages and presented a haunch of veal. 'Compliments of the *Das Reich* food kitchen! Apparently, we received a huge amount of supplies today, more than usual so I wonder what's afoot. I did hear that our Abwher (intelligent services) had picked up heavy wireless traffic on large troop movements in England, mainly towards Dover. That's a long way from here, too far for us to intervene so that will have to be dealt with by Von Rundstedt if the invasion comes there.'

'Maybe it won't come at all' said Wilhelm, 'We have an impregnable Atlantic wall.'

'Yes, replied Wolfie, but I think the battles will be won in the air. So don't expect our Luftwaffe to be getting off their backsides.'

Wolfie turned his attention to Yvette and Yves. 'So, what have my little prince and princess been doing today?'

'I am not your princess', replied Yvette tartly, 'in fact this princess wants a word with you in private.' At that comment mama's eyes opened wide and her mouth fell open, but no words came.

Yves however was full of himself; 'today I helped in the garage, apparently you Germans are stealing our cars now so there was a lot to do. I know how to take an engine apart, well at least how to replace a piston. When I get a car, I will be able to do all the repairs on it!'

'No one is stealing anything' said Wolfie, 'it's called requisitioning transport for military purposes. It's on loan to the Reich. What car was it?'

'A beautiful open top Mercedes belonging to count Barfleur who lives in the chateau near Limoges; I am sure he is sad to see it go'

"Sounds like that will be for general Lammerding, 'said Wolfie. "But I wouldn't travel in that, not with all those Spitfires around!'

Mama cooked the veal. Wolfie produced a bottle of schnapps and soon the two pals were well away, starting to sing German songs. Yves played with his drumsticks. Yvette was quiet and sullen. Mama busied herself and tried not to think the worst.

MAY 31ST 1944

It was a hot night, and although the moon was not quite yet at its fullest, it seemed to penetrate the broken wood of the shutters and illuminate the rooms like daylight. Mama dozed fitfully. The meal had been a great success and for once they all felt full. But she could not help putting meat onto the bones of Yvette's little outburst. She kept thinking 'what if?' 'What if the father was not Pascal. That was too terrible to contemplate. She took a big swig of cognac from the secret supply by her bed and fell asleep snoring loudly.

Raoul was as tidy as he could be with his sidings. They were full. Hans said he had a bad feeling in his bones that much carnage would come to all the freshly painted tanks on their rail cars. 'They are lined up waiting for destruction' he muttered. True, if the allies bombed the sidings, they were a perfect target, but allied bombing had not come as far south as Montauban. It was concentrated around Poitiers and the important rail junctions further north. The Panther tanks were all covered in camouflage netting making them difficult to see from the sky, but it only needed one spy to tell the allies otherwise. The moon was glinting on anything steel, almost saying 'look at what I can see, no blanket of darkness can hide my light!'

Terri and her brothers had stopped all night-time movements of arms and people – there was no darkness to hide under and the countryside was laid out like a bright reflective chequered quilt, exposing anything that moved.

Most of the *Das Reich* personnel preferred to sleep out in the open underneath their trucks and tanks, but Wolfie and Wilhelm liked the comfort of a proper bed with clean sheets. They knew this would not last, so they made the most of it.

Claude and Jenny were stuck; she could not send signals because the atmosphere was full of crackle and interference and Claude was unable to travel under cover of darkness to his next training session.

The heat was coming out of Spain and rolling in waves up the hills of the Correze getting to everyone, making them irritable, it was unseasonably hot at 33c daytime and 30c at night.

Forty- Four

SYLVIE NO MORE

JUNE 1ˢᵀ 1944, MOON 75% WEATHER HUMID AND STORMY

'Les sanglots longs, Des violons, De l'automne'
The Germans wrongly believed that these lines were addressed to all Resistance circuits in France, and that when the next three lines were broadcast it would mean that invasion would follow within forty-eight hours, the lines were directed to a single Resistance circuit, Ventriloquist, working south of Orléans, instructing it to stand by for the next three lines, which would be the signal for it to carry out its railway-cutting tasks — in conjunction with the Allied landings."

Although directed to one circuit, it wasn't long before the news spread like wildfire to other circuits down the Correze, Dordogne and South into Montauban. Terri heard it first and ran to the café 'Rudi, its starting soon. Within forty-eight hours! Soon the whole town knew it, including Wolfie and Wilhelm who were lubricating their tanks. General Lammerding gathered his senior staff together,

"I will find out from Berlin what their preliminary orders are. No one yet knows where they will land but apart from this horrible cloudy weather today, we are in fine fettle and ready for anything. Pass the word for confinement to barracks for all ranks except for those officers living within 2 kilometers.'

Yvette heard it from Yves and there was mild excitement in the household. And he scurried round next door but Madelaine, kneading her dough on the table, was more sanguine saying that she wanted proof not poems before she would believe it. Too many times before there had been false starts. 'What 'ever the little brother plans to do, don't go running around with Rabbit Girl.'

'Ah but Terri wants me to meet her today anyway so I will let you know' he said with a poutful grin.' He disappeared but a few hours later came running in saying 'It's you Terri wants to meet urgently' pointing his finger at Yvette.

JUNE 2ND 1944

Pascal was sweating, as were the three other men in his cell into which he had been thrown the day before. He had had nothing to drink since last night and hunger was excruciating, his stomach protesting vigorously. At 9 am some bread and water were brought to them all and they drank copiously and ate sparingly. Then a German officer with a guard came, unlocked the cell, and motioned Pascal up the steps into a corridor and an office. Behind the desk sat a Gestapo colonel who invited Pascal to sit down. Then the questioning started. It was all polite because the colonel invited to Pascal to speak in German or French. Pascal chose German as he wanted to distance himself as far as possible from the maquisards he had teamed up with after the car crash. He repeated his story, again narrowing the timeline to two days. The Colonel said 'Look, I don't doubt your story, it's a very good one, but you have no proof or witnesses. I would like to believe that as a good German from Alsace you want to fight for the Reich, but maybe you are just a deserter, or even worse a terrorist' Pascal denied both. Then the door opened, and Hugo was brought in, his face bruised and bloody. 'Do you know each other? came the question. They both denied knowing each other. Then another door opened, and a little old lady was brought in. Pascal immediately recognised her, and his heart sank. She was the lady who had questioned Sylvie as to where she had obtained the drugs.

'Do you recognise these men? Asked the Colonel. 'Yes sir, she replied these are two of the men who brought me medicines. A thin smile creased the colonel's mouth. "so, you are the Frenchman who speaks German and was part of the raid on the pharmacy. I am so sorry, but I had hoped it would turn out differently as we need every good Alsatian to fight for the Reich, but you have blown your cover. Take them away.'

They were both led away back to the same cell. 'What happened?" asked Pascal. 'We were betrayed by the very people we were trying to help, maybe for money or just out of spite. Who knows?" Where are the others?

Asked Pascal 'The men have already been shipped out to Germany. I was brought from the train at the platform when they knew they had you, to identify you.' "What about Sylvie?' asked Pascal. 'Sorry Pascal, She is dead. They knew she was the ringleader and they shot her on the spot when we were captured. Not before she had killed three of them, she put up a good fight, and would have killed more but her sten gun jammed.'

Pascal was silent. He was thinking of that warm lithe soft girly body he had made love to. All the nurture and growth of a fine young woman with ideals and optimism now no more. He let out a big sigh. Now, just a dead pile of bones somewhere. 'And us? What are they going to do?' 'I think we are going to be shipped to Germany as well, as slaves for work,' said Hugo. 'Otherwise, they would have shot us by now'

Forty-Five

THE SABOTAGE

JUNE 3ᴿᴰ 1944

Back in Montauban the thunderstorm that burst following the hot weather brought rain and darkness to the city. Terri sent a message to Yvette that she needed help tonight and to meet her at the café at 5pm. Yvette had an early supper and, although not keen on this venture, was there at the appointed hour. Terri was sitting in the corner and when Yvette sat down whispered that tonight was the night for their clandestine operation.

'First we have to leave here before curfew and slip into the marshalling yards and hide underneath the signal box where the workmen store their tools. There will be a supply of grinding paste and under cover of darkness and the weather we will pour the grinding paste into the axels of the low loaders carrying the tanks and heavy artillery. Just one axel per unit will suffice. That way after a few miles the wheels on the wagons will seize up."

'You're crazy,' said Yvette. 'there will be guards and dogs. We will be caught'

'Not if we are clever; I have already been told that due to the weather and torrential rain expected in the next few hours the guards will be a skeleton crew and as for the dogs, they will be set free, running loose; we have concocted a very tasty sweet meat laced into a raisin cake with a strong sedative – the opposite of Pervitin widely used by the Wehrmacht to keep them awake and a very strong sedative based on a morphine derivative. This was developed by our tame chemist. It will keep the dog asleep or dozy for an hour."

'First how will you catch the dog?'

'They will already be drowsy; dogs hate thunder and static electricity; their handlers will already have given them a calming chew and a safe place about an hour before we go in. So, if one does appear our raisin cake will just be a dessert!'

'How do you know about the handlers?' asked Yvette.

"One of the handlers has befriended a girl friend of mine; there is nothing she doesn't know about these Nazi dogs and how they handle them.'

'What can go wrong? It sounds risky. We could be shot'

"look, you want to do something for Pascal, I want to do something for France. All our information from the resistance is that the allies will land in the next seventy-two hours.; we wouldn't be surprised if the *Das Reich* starts to move withing forty-eight hours. So, this is our best chance. Are you with me?'

Reluctantly Yvette said yes.

'Good, in the store there will be warm clothes and

blankets, we will be soaking wet by midnight. We lie low in the store until dawn. Then creep out and run.

It was beginning, the biggest storm Yvette had ever seen. After a record temperature of 40degrees that engulfed the Dordogne, all the southwest was washed with lashing rain, huge rolling thunder and lightning bolts that seemed to come from hell rather than heaven. The noise was frightening, and all the sheep, cows, cats, and dogs ran for safety. Babies cried. The troopers of the *Das Reich* hungered down in their lagers, the officers including General Lammerding closed the shutters in their Chapeau. The resistance curtailed all expeditions. No one was arrested or shot that night. It was as though the armies of mankind bowed before the supernatural wrath of the heavens and just simply stayed indoors.

'Good, said Terri. Perfect for us, but we will get wet.' They made their way to the marshalling yards, no sentry challenged them, they couldn't even see the tracks for the rain. Terri pulled on the door of the little cabin. It wouldn't open. 'I hope it's not locked; just pull hard,' said Yvette. Terri pulled and the wood creaked loudly, then it opened. 'Must have swelled with the rain' she said. Inside they dried themselves a bit and organised the raid on the wagons. 'we have enough here for 20 flatbeds, we'll do ten each, you on one track and me on another. Choose the ones with tanks on, don't worry about other vehicles. Just put the powder into one tank on one axel only. Pour and move. Pour and move. With luck it will take us half an hour.' Said Terri. There was a terrific clap of thunder right over head Montauban; upstairs in the signal box Rudi and Raoul almost jumped out of their skins. It was now eight pm. They had heard no noise from downstairs in the cabin. 'I don't like this' said Raoul. I am going to ring command and tell them we are closing for the night. Stop all inbound trains. Command in Periguex wasn't concerned; all over the region electricity was out, poles were down, tracks flooded. A signal box in Montauban was the least of the railway's problems tonight. They got the agreement to go home. Raoul pulled all levers to stop. Then they and their sullen guard left the box and went home.

Terri heard them go. In fact, she had forgotten they were there. Good job the thunder had hid the noise of the creaking door.

Half an hour went by, and Terri said 'time to go. Come on. Keep low. We both have a pouch with the powder in and in you left pocket some special cakes for the dogs. They both slid out, dressed in black outfits from the cabin, they had blackened their faces with wet soot and pulled a balaclava on their heads. Yvette chose the nearest siding and Terri the one next to it. Yvette looked up at the huge tank looming above her and for a moment wondered if this was Wolfie's tank. Putting it out of action would save him from death. Maybe. She went to work. Pour and move. Terri had reached the third car when she heard a dog bark. She froze. Nothing happened then it barked again, closer now. She slowly edged the cake from her pocket and the long hunting knife she used for skinning rabbits from her trouser legging. She had not told Yvette about the ultimate deterrent of killing the dog with one upward slice across its throat. She kept dead still then felt the dark shape of a dog nuzzling up to her sniffing at the cake. She opened her palm, let the dog sniff and then it gulped down the cake. She felt it safe enough to stroke its head. Then she gave it a second cake. The dog lay down munching and Terri continued to flatbed four. That dog will be asleep in five minutes, the heavy sedative laced with morphine would do its work, she thought.

It was 9m when they had both finished the sabotage. They were so wet they almost were swimming. The rain kept pounding down. Terri and Yvette crawled back into their little hut, took off their wet clothes and rubbed themselves vigorously with towels. Yvette was shivering from fright as much as cold. Terri wrapped herself then wrapped Yvette inside her blanket with her. Yvette's teeth were chattering.

When I heard the dog, I was so frightened, I froze,' said Yvette. 'It was fortunate that there was huge clap of thunder when the dog barked, nobody would have heard it. Good job because I was wrong about the dog not liking thunder; it behaved normally. Must have been the army training, just like the sound of battle. Anyway, we got away with it,' said Terri. 'Now if they move those wagons the axels will seize up after a few kilometers.'

'Maybe that will save lives from going to the hell of war,' said Yvette.

Hell is where we will all end up', said Terri. 'Heaven is here on earth; it's now, it's here today; that's why the garden of Eden was created; god chose this earth to be Eden with trees and fruits, grains and animals, rivers and oceans. Heaven is what we make of it, there is no second heaven. Only the hell of eternal darkness' said Terri.

Yvette was startled' 'that can't be true' our pastors and

priests have been telling us in school that heaven and hell come after this life. Where did you get this idea from? Said Yvette.

'To me it's perfectly logical; there is no after life; its heaven now, family life, love and enjoyment, nature, all what we make of it'

Just then an enormous clap of thunder shook the signal box. More lightening flashed through the cracks in the door; and the rain fell in solid sheets.

They hugged each other and went to sleep.

JUNE 4ᵀᴴ 1944

During the storms of the previous day and all through the 4th the BBC sent the personal messages to the Maquis. The first few lines the poem of the long sobs of autumn were broadcast. Jenni picked it up.

'Les Sanglots longs
Des violins
De l'automne'

'Aha' said Claude' That means they will land within 48 hours. But where?

Although they didn't know it, those lines were destined to a specific Resistance circuit ('Ventriloquist') south of Orleans; but every resistance group heard it. So did the Germans. General Lammerding was not perturbed. Without firm information what was he to believe. He was virtually besieged by the maquis who roamed at will across the Correze, Dordogne and Lot. His preoccupation was to keep his army safe and contained until he received firm orders from OKW (German high command) but he decided to get the trains loaded up and moving out of the sidings.

The wires were beginning to hum with rumour and excitement.

The day had begun well, the sun was hot, the storm had passed through. Terri and Yvette were dry and quietly opened the door of the cabin. The vision was like volcano sending masses of steam into the air as the hot sun vaporised the moisture off the wet silver tracks and the wagons in the sidings. The air was damp, but the sun would soon burn off the vapour. They used the two bicycles stored in the cabin and wheeled them calmly up and out of the sidings. It was then that they were stopped by the German officer pointing his Luger 9mm pistol at them and shouting that they were saboteurs and threatening to shoot them.

Terri, bold as life and twiddling her long hair had smiled at him and said' we were out for a bike ride last night and got caught in the storm. We sheltered in the signal box cabin

And it was then that the SS Colonel had intervened and told the captain that these were only schoolgirls and that he should preserve his strength for fighting the Americans. He told them to run home and stay there. Little did they know what Terri and Yvette had been doing during the night.

Back home Yvette's mother was clearly upset. "Where were you all night?' she asked. Yvette explained that she had visited Terri at the farm, got caught in the storm and stayed the night there. Yves seemed to know that his sister had been up to no good but said nothing.

Just then Wolfie came down the stairs dressed in full battle gear.

'Hello everybody, we have been put on full alert and we may be moving off tomorrow. Here are my ration cards for you, all the officers are doing the same, and a hundred Francs I had kept for a special occasion, but I won't be needing them here anymore. From today I am consigned to my unit and will live with my men'

"where will you sleep' burst out Yvette.

'well, my tank is big enough to sleep in, but we all prefer to sleep outside underneath the tank for shelter and away from danger, don't worry about me little princess. Maybe one day I will come back and see you again. Madam, and the little Rascal Yves, I thank you all so much for being so kind to me and sharing your food. I regret no more rabbit stew though! And Yvette you can have your bed back and keep playing the piano, that's a memory I shall treasure.

'Just a minute, said Yvette. She ran upstairs and came down with a little leather thong that held a badge. 'This is a St Christophe necklace, it's a symbol of safe travel and protection. It's really meant for mariners to keep them safe from the sea but I want you to have it to keep you safe for me'

Wolfie smiled his broad grin and kissed Yvette on the cheek. "I shall wear it always' he said.

'Now I must go, and by the way, Wilhelm sends his love.'

All over Montauban the men of the *Das Reich* were saying goodbye to their lodgings, girlfriends and Rudi at the café said "Now I can bring out my good wines'. 'Don't be too hasty said his wife. 'They haven't gone yet, and Germans have a nasty habit of returning!

Andre Malraux and Le Rat were in high spirits as the rumours spread. 'From now on all the men must be ready with their guns' said Andre. 'And as soon as we know where the allies have landed, then we will block the routs out of here and harass the Germans at every step. Le Rat, get a message to Claude to ask London for one more shipment drop as quickly as possible."

Forty-Six

EXCITING NEWS

JUNE 6TH 1944 FULL MOON

Pascal was taken from the cells along with Hugo and thirty other captives and marched to the station at Poitier. They were herded to the end of the platform where cattle trucks stood. Men and women were being pushed at gun point into the wagons. Soon Pascal and Hugo were prodded and shoved still wearing handcuffs into an evil smelling car. The cuffs were then taken off by a surly foul-smelling corporal. But as they had scrambled up the plank into the wagon, Pascal noticed a word scrawled in chalk on its side. One menacing word that sent shivers down his spine: Dachau

Claude was wakened at 2am by Jenny who punched him in the ribs.

'Ouch, what was that for? He growled.

'Wake up wake up, the second verse of the poem has been transmitted, you know, the Paul Verlaine poem,

'Blessent mon coeur
D'une langueur
Monotone'
Now we have the full poem
'Les sanglots longs
Des violins
De l'automne'

The first verse we had on July 1st to warn us the invasion was imminent. Now the second part means it's under way! This is wonderful news. Oh, and by the way, your personal message came through

'It's hot in Cairo'

Claude woke with a jolt. The poem was one thing, but his own personal message confirmed the landings were happening.

'Do we know where?' He asked

'No, not yet but by morning we will. How exciting!'

'yes, and very dangerous! As soon as the Germans know they may be very trigger happy so we must stay hidden'

No, she said, we must go down to the town this morning and report on any movements.'

'Yes, you are right' said Claude but we can sleep a little more, we can't go down at this hour.'

By the time they were decently awake at 0830 and able to tell madam le grange the good news, she had already heard it on the BBC bulletin that the allies had landed in Normandy.

'So that's it, they have landed nearly 700 kilometers

away from the South of France. I wonder how the *Das Reich* are going to get there and by when. We must try and find out as much as we can this morning.'

General Lammerding heard the news from OKW about 0900. The report was that the intelligence suggested this might be a decoy and that the real landings were going to happen at the Pas de Calais. He called Field Marshall von Rundstedt who said 'The fools in Berlin still think it's the wrong place; Rommel is convinced it's the real thing and has requested that the Panzers be released. But Hitler is still asleep, can't be woken, so we are helpless. If they establish a bridgehead, we will be too late to counterattack. And you must wait on orders to march.'

Lammerding was flabbergasted. It was only a 3-day journey by rail, if they could get enough trains. His command team estimated they would need seventy trains. He decided to ignore orders and get his 15,000 men and 450 tanks, some of them the latest mark 2 Tigers, started. He issued his own orders to mobilise.

Terri heard then news from Rudi at the café. The maquis were spreading the news like wildfire. At last, it would be open season on the hated Bosch. Yvette and Yves heard the news, like everyone else in Montauban, by mid-day. The noise of excitement was at full volume.

Raoul, working away in his signal box, was told to get 70 locomotives ready. "They are mad, where will I find 70 locomotives! I have got 5 here, 4 more at Poitier and maybe six at Angouleme. If they haven't all been sabotaged, I can get 15 trains away tomorrow but 70, impossible. Maybe in three weeks but this morning I heard a lot of the lines have been blown up already. The railway is a complete mess.

Hans smiled, that all knowing smile that said 'It's too late'

But the division started to stir up from its slumber, like a giant beast awakening. Soon, the infantry was marching to the rendezvous point. Yves and Yvette heard them singing as they marchcd.

"What are the singing? asked Yves. 'A bystander replied 'it's the Horst vessel song' better known as *Der Fahne Hoch*. The flag is high.

'It's a pretty song and a good one to march to' said Yves, who was impressed by the drums, bugles, big brass band and flags. 'What does it mean?' 'well said the bystander, I am from Alsace, so I know its folklore mixed with Nazi words from the Munich days of brownshirts and the rise of the Nazi party. It has a lot of verses but some of the words are:

The flag is high, our ranks are closed
The S.A. marches with silent solid steps.
Comrades shot by the red front and reaction
March in spirit with us in our ranks.
The street is free for the brown battalions

At the mention of Alsace, Yvette's heart missed more than a beat. She thought of Pascal. Where was he. Was he still alive? The questions pounded her whole body louder than the big bass drum beating out the marching steps.

'It's very exciting,' said Yves.

Yvette cuffed him across the back of the head. 'You stupid boy, these are Germans. The enemy of France.'

'All these girls and women waving at them don't think that, they like them?' said Yves

'Most of them have been Nazi whores, who slept with the Germans, they will be beaten up and disgraced when the Germans have left"

'Are you a Nazi whore?' Asked Yves

Yvette hit him again 'Don't ever ask me that again, of course I'm not'

'Well, what about Wolfie?' said Yves – Terri told me you had an affair with him. And you gave him the St Christophe medal.

Yvette broke into tears and ran home to her bedroom, now empty but for the smell of Wolfie's cologne and the impression of his body on the bed.

Claude and Jenny watched the procession of soldiers, trucks, and armoured vehicles marching to the rendezvous point just outside Montauban where they would have to wait for orders. They couldn't help but feel impressed by the powerful display of men and materials. Claude noticed a lot of soldiers with the flash on their arms denoting the Alsace regiment, what would come to be known as *"Malgre Nous'* (conscripted men 'against our will'). Claude told Jenny felt he had to get to see Andre Malraux and Le rat but where would they be? It would be chaos and dangerous to move around.

'Claude, you can't possibly think of trying to find them, there will be plenty of maquis wanting to take a pot shot at these soldiers and they have no hope of fighting combat soldiers who will react violently as they are trained to do. Let's just report back to London that the '*Das Reich*' is preparing to move' she said. Reluctantly Claude agreed.

Forty-Eight

MOSQUITO RECSUE

BAKER STREET

A message came through from the small band of SOE agents who had landed near Poitier to provide reconnaissance for bombing the marshalling yards at Poitier. They could clearly see the yards stacked with wagons, and more importantly, petrol tankers. But they also warned against collateral damage to the inhabitants as the yards were close into the town.

Buckmaster called his team together and they decided on a low-level airstrike.

'There is only one aircraft that can get in low and fast and that's a squadron of mosquitos, so Jim, please get onto coastal command and request immediate assistance. They must attack in the next hour this morning and target the petrol tankers.'

Pascal was wakened very early that morning in the cattle wagon by the sound of aircraft. It had been a terrible night. One old man was dead. Someone had kicked over toilet bucket. The fresh drinking water had been drunk. The noise grew louder. Suddenly the whole car was lifted into the air by a giant explosion. "That's not just a bombe' said Hugo who fell on top of Pascal and they both fell into the mucky slime on the floor.

The cattle truck fell back down on the track. But its sides were splintered open. "Quick, we can prise these planks apart. Hugo with his immense strength caved in the side of the wagon. 'C'mon, let's go'

Pascal Hugo and twenty other survivors tumbled out onto the tracks. What they saw nearly blinded them. A huge petrol train had been blown up about 200 hundred metres behind them on another track. Hugo spotted the roundels like bulls eye targets on the side of the planes —'It's the English RAF!' he shouted — those are RAF Mosquitos, twin engine, beautiful, very fast'. By now Pascal knew Hugo to be an expert on all things military but now was not the time to hang around. The droves of planes were still attacking the marshalling yards and trains at Poitier.

The heat was intense, Pascal and Hugo shielded their faces as they ran, they ran anywhere in the darkness. 'We have got to get out of the station complex,' said Pascal. 'Let's head for the outskirts of the town. We have got to head south. This is the second time the English flyers have saved my life, first the spitfire and second these low flying Mosquitos, so low and fast like bats out of hell. Now I intend to make it home to my parents, my farm, and the girl I adore.'

'Can I come with you?' said Hugo 'I have nowhere else to go.

"Yes of course, when we get to the farm, we will restock it and you can help me plough the lower forty, you're big and strong enough to pull the plough yourself! C'mon gentle giant, run like you've never run before'

The stopped suddenly at a water fountain and gulped down bucket loads of clean fresh water, then they splashed it all over themselves to wash away some of the stink of the rail car.

'Quick, that's enough, said Pascal. 'Down this street here, follow the tram lines'

The streets of Poitier were full of people running, not just escapees from the train, but ordinary residents whose houses were burning. It seemed the English Mosquitos were intent on destroying the whole town, its road and rail network and any Germans they could. But the collateral damage for the French was horrible. Many were killed in their beds by stray bombes.

The Germans were also running in panic. Poitiers had been bombed many times but not like this. This time it was different.

General Lammerding was pacing up and down, waiting for orders to move. The orders didn't arrive for another forty-eight hours.

Forty-Nine

MISSION IMPOSSIBLE

JUNE 8TH

A fter D Day, Claude received a top –secret communique from London. SOE Baker street wanted him to travel to Sussac in the Haut Vienne and meet a new English SOE courier and take her to liase with the Maquis in the Correze and Dordogne and to coordinate the resistance groups in the west. Her code name was 'Louise' and the password 'The life that I have' and the response 'the life that I have is yours'.

'This is very dangerous said Jenny – we know that the Maquis leader in Sussac is an ardent communist and not disposed to London or the British.'

"Yes, that's why I have to help get her out from there. She is no use to us in the Sussac'.

'But it's a long way from here, over 100 miles. And we know the *Das Reich* is on the move. It will be like tangling with a boa constrictor.'

"I can take the train"

'It will be full of soldiers'

'That's the point, I won't stand out and be noticed. I shall go alone in my capacity as a Bordeaux Wine salesman. Send a message through London to have someone meet me tomorrow at St-Germain-Les-Belles — that's only 30 minutes from Sussac — I shall have a red rose in my button-hole'

"I still don't think it's a good idea,' said Jenny. "You know that more and more couriers and agents are picked up and your priceless asset is luck; you have had a good run so far and our network here hasn't been brutally penetrated not like Limoges or Lyons, but the war has moved to us, and you have only got to touch the wrong contact and it's fatal. All these bourgeoisie French people who have lived a life of compromise, live and let live, are now starving, desperate and threatened by an army that is no longer a peaceful occupier, who have now become the hunted so it's an explosive mix. The Germans let the resistance exist as a romantic political necessity but now Madam la Grange tells me French people are rushing to join the resistance and doing stupid things; you don't want to get caught in the middle."

'I know' said Claude 'but according to London this courier is going to link up with one of our top agents in the Lot and Garonne and needs our help on the ground. There are too many untrustworthy maquis in Sussac.'

Claude walked into Montauban and was amazed at the activity. Lorries, soldiers still everywhere. He wasn't stopped or accosted and went to the Train Station to get a return ticket for Limoges. He wasn't going as far as that as the plan was to get off the train at St–Germain-Les-Belles.

There were only two trains to stop at Les-Belles, so he chose the departure at 12 noon. The booking clerk said 'Messieurs, there will be a lot of delays tomorrow as the Wehrmacht has commandeered many engines and trains. It would be safer to take the 1000hrs train for Limoges. 'Does that stop at Le -Belles?' The clerk looked at him with suspicion, 'yes but there is nothing there he said.'

'I have an old aunt I need to see,' said Claude. 'Ah yes, always and old aunt' retorted the clerk and passed him the ticket. 'Make sure your travel passes are in order'

JUNE 11TH

Claude went early to the station wearing his bowler hat and suit with the red rose given him by Madam La Grange and pinned on, somewhat lovingly Claude thought, by Jenny.

He bought a baguette and water at the Café Flaubert, exchanging conversation with Rudi.

'Where are our Gestapo friends?' 'They have gone, for the moment but sadly always they have a habit of coming back' said Rudi. 'They have ransacked the town of any valuables or art, loaded them on wagons destined for Germany and disappeared. They know that it's too dangerous now to stay here.'

'How do you know this?' said Claude.

'You see that girl and that man in the corner? They are maquis; the girl is called Terri; a tough fighter and the man is Etienne, her ami; Terri was involved the other night in jamming the freight car axels with grinding paste. They moved a few hundred metres then seized up."

'I need a favour said Claude' do you know an old lady in Germain -le-belles? I need an excuse to get off the train there.' Rudi thought and said' the postmistress is a friend of mine. She is called Vivien Bertrand and lives above the post office.'

Claude thanked him and moved to the station platform. It was jammed with soldiers, mostly women with babies and chickens in baskets and a few old men. The train came in from Toulouse and with only 5 coaches was so crowded that Claude had to stand, at least as far as Brive. It was very hot. Claude was sweating profusely after an hour. At Brive, some sinister men wearing black trench coats got on; they smelled of Gestapo. Claude inched his way closer to the door, just in case. The train moved with a jolt and threw everyone together. As a result, he fell against a young woman. He could smell her perfume mixed with sweat; slightly intoxicating he thought. 'Pardon Mademoiselle. 'Pas de soucis, le train est très bondé' she replied, smiling. 'Ou allez-vous ?'. 'Moi, je vais au les belles pour voir ma tante' she said. Claude couldn't believe his luck; just then the Gestapo pushed between them asking for papers which they both produced. 'Where are you going? 'the big brutish one said 'She replied I am going to Germain-le-belles to see my aunt' she said. He looked quizzically at her. 'What is in the basket?' he said. She took off the napkin and uncovered the basket. There was bread, ham, apples, cheese and a bottle of wine' 'That's quite a picnic; I think it's from the black market which is illegal' he said. 'No, it's all bought with my saved coupons' she said smiling at him. Claude felt uneasy but the girl was as calm as a cucumber. He gave her papers back, said nothing then turned to Claude who was now sweating profusely. 'Your papers say you are a wine salesman, who-ever wants to buy wine during a war' he grunted. 'well, our best customers are Germans' said Claude. 'Where are you going? Was the reply. "I am going to Poitiers where I have good hotels with lots of German clients. They need my good Bordeaux wine there.' Claude then twisted his bow tie to lie flat. If the German thought he was sweating too much he didn't say so; everyone was sweating; it was a hot day. His documents were returned, and he moved on. The girl looked at him and said 'I thought you were going to les belles?' Claude smiled 'well I have to see an old aunt there as well' he said. He could see she did not believe him. However, everyone had a right to their secrets she thought. They talked about wine. The train moved on slowly. Now and again, it was diverted into a loop as a military train thundered past going north. Finally, they arrived at Germain- les – belles. They both got off together and walked to the pretty station exit still talking as they passed the scrutiny of the Germans at the barrier. Outside, Claude said 'may I know your name please?' 'It's Florian' she said' and, good luck messieurs, whatever you are doing here' she said with a twinkle in her eye.

There was a black Citroen parked against the hedge. Claude slowly walked towards it as a young man jumped out and said, 'The life that I have' … and Claude replied. 'is yours and yours' passwords exchanged he said 'can I give you a lift to Sussac'? My name is Anastasie. 'Yes of course' said Claude. 'Tell me has your boss arrived?' Yes, the night before last, June 7; a parachute drop, at

St–Gilles–les–Forets near Mont Gargan and the village of Sardou Sérénité, so she is safe and in good hands.

"and her name?'

'it's Corinne but also known as Louise, or La petite Anglaise because she is small. Tomorrow June 10th we leave for the Dordogne' 'You realise that the Germans are on the march; the *Das Reich* division is headed for Normandie so we must be careful to avoid them' said Claude.

'There aren't any around here; we had a few patrols the other night which delayed some parachute drops but where we are is perfectly safe. Here in Maquis country, we can roam at will, we have thousands of fighters now, even the hated Milice are deserting and joining us. The Germans tend to stay clear of us around here.'

Claude was amazed at how arrogant and frivolous everyone was. Maybe everything would go swimmingly. He had heard from London that Anastasie had a price on his head; the Germans were desperate to catch him for he was renowned for the sabotage in the Limoges area.

They arrived at the safe house in Sussac. There Claude met the four agents who had been parachuted in. They sat down to supper. 'I hope they are looking after you,' said Claude. It was Corinne who answered first 'I am being treated like royalty, breakfast in bed, no food to cook and total relaxation. We can't go out of course, they are being very careful.'

'And the drop?' said Claude

'Perfect; the flight was noisy with lots of flack over Normandie, there were no seats so the deck was hard for the four hours but the Liberator is a big plane, and we were carrying lots of armaments and supplies for the maquis so it was amazing that everything including us could be dropped almost together. Well, no, actually, we jumped first then the Liberator made a second pass for the supplies and our cases. Just before I hit the ground, I felt strong arms around my legs pulling me down; for an instant I thought they might be German, but I was then smothered in kisses and helped me out of my harness. What a welcome; It took over an hour to clear the landing site. They brought a big lorry for the supplies and a car for us.'

With Corrinne was a radio operator, an American liaison officer and her boss Charles. They were all in high spirits, laughing, joking, and enjoying the copious wine that flowed. Claude couldn't help thinking how beautiful Corrinne was, jet black hair and high cheekbones; in conversation she revealed that her husband had been killed at El Alamein in North Africa in 1942 and she wanted to do something to help avenge him. This was her second mission. Her mother was French so of course she spoke fluent French. She had also left behind at home a three -year daughter, Tania. Claude wondered why such a beautiful mother of 23 would want to put herself in such danger; she ran the considerable risk of never seeing Tania again.

They talked about the mission; Claude was to ensure that Corrine was got safely to the Dordogne, the Corrèze Maquis, but they had to pass through the Creuse Maquis to the east who were not to be trusted. At all costs they had to avoid all roads around Limoges which being a heavy armaments town was blockaded with special passes being needed. They would drive south then southwest. Philip, the boss of the local maquis said 'Anastasie will take you to meet the Correze head man to give credibility to your mission and to deliver the plan for all the maquis in the area to forget their rivalries and join up to help prevent the *Das Reich* getting to Normandie; there will be 3,000 maquisards if we all act together but we must have Anastasie back, he is the master of the operation here.'

Corrine nodded and Anastasie said he would be back in four hours adding the *Das Reich* will never get through. Claude again cautioned them all saying that direct force would be suicide, that they had to stick to sabotage. That was what SOE London wanted.

'Why are we driving. A car with us all in will arouse suspicion, surely its best to go by bicycle especially as the Germans have banned the use of cars since D-day?' said Claude.

'We need to drive in comfort and get there quickly. We have made special arrangements for fuel; we have plenty of petrol, and don't be worried, I know this area very well because I grew up here. There are no Germans for miles around'

JUNE 10, 1944

The three of them got in the car; Anastasie suggested Claude drive, he sat beside him to navigate, with guns and grenades on their laps in case of trouble; Corrinne sat in the back with her Sten gun and nine magazines in a rucksack. At nine thirty they set off on the D 2087 la route de Meilhards, and in the warm morning sun they all felt happy. They headed for Salon-la- Tour where they had to cross the main road to Limoges. Anastasie said that was where he grew up, so he knew all the little side roads. Claude was apprehensive but shared in the conversation and banter. Just outside Salon-la-Tour, Claude slowed almost to a halt. He could see the scissor arrangements of a road- block ahead with two Germans on guard

'I thought you said there were no Germans here' said Claude to Anastasie. 'They shouldn't be here; what the hell are they doing and why are they here? He replied.' We have two options' said Claude speaking fast; turn around and go back risking some shots; or drive through the roadblock – there's only two soldiers there.

'let's drive through them – keep your head down Corrinne but prime your gun' said Anastasie. Corrinne cocked her sten gun.

Claude put his foot flat to the floor and the accelerated forward towards the two Germans.

Captain Schmidt of the Grenadier Regiment Deutschland was having a quite smoke. He and his 200 men had been searching for his commanding officer Major Kamphe who had been captured by the maquis. The regiment had bivouacked behind the trees and set up a roadblock. Schmidt was startled to see the car hurtling towards them. He opened fire and the car slewed into the ditch. Anastasie and Corrine leapt from the car, she with rucksack over her shoulders. Anastasie ran one way and Corrine the other, into an orchard. They had stirred up a wasp's nest. Claude was slumped over the wheel, shot through the head. Anastasie was never seen again, hiding under a woodpile until nightfall. Corrine ran through the orchard firing from the hip. Then she stumbled and fell over a tree root, an old parachute injury to her ankle. She turned and sprayed the orchard with her sten gun, catching several soldiers running after her. But by now the whole regiment had tumbled out of their wagons and were in hot pursuit. Corrine dragged herself behind an apple tree and methodically emptied magazine after magazine at her pursuers until all nine magazines in her rucksack were gone. It was clear they wanted her alive. Captain Schmidt approached, he holstered his gun, he looked at the beautiful women, her face streaked with black, and her blue dress torn, who had collapsed at his feet and smiled 'congratulations madam, that was a hell of a fight,' he said in perfect English. He offered her a cigarette, which she promptly refused. One of the soldiers gave her a drink of water which she gladly accepted. 'You are very brave' he said 'but sadly we haven't time to make your acquaintance further. I am on a mission to find my commanding officer so I will have to hand you over to the Gestapo. I am sorry to say you will not find the same courtesy from them.' Two soldiers carefully helped her to her feet and carried her to their wagon and drove off towards Gestapo headquarters in Limoges. There the Gestapo discovered her real identity, it was Violet Szabo, of British SOE. They realised what a prize they had and made immediate arrangements for her transfer to Gestapo headquarters in Paris.

Fifty

THE MARCH TO NORMANDY BEGINS AND TERRI HAS TROUBLE BREWING

JUNE 8TH 1944

Yvette was still upset with her brother. She went to speak with Terri and questioned her on what she had said to Yves.

'He asked me if I knew anything about you and the Nazi officer, I just said I thought you were fond of him. Nothing more. He is just inventing things. Only you and I know the truth and we have sworn a pact together, remember?'

'Yes, I remember. If anything happens to me, please look after him for me'

'Nothing is going to happen to you. I heard this morning that the *'Das Reich'* will finally be on the move north today, so soon they will all be gone. Happy days will return.' Said Terri.

Raoul was busy in the signal box. He was marshalling engines, which had been in steam for two days, onto the low loaders with the tanks on board. Hans was helping him pull levers. The first train started to move, straining under the heavy load. It passed the signal box and picked up speed. Soldiers on the wagons were shouting and waving at the town's folk. It had reached the bridge over the river when a terrible screeching noise of metal on metal was heard, the soldiers covered their ears. The engine driver noticed the drop in speed and slowed down to a stop. A captain on the rear wagon got down and ordered his men off the train. The wheels of the wagons were smoking.

'Quick, get the engineer here, bring oil for the wheels.' He shouted. The engineers appeared and inspected the wheel bearings. 'They are kaput, we can't get oil into them because they are locked solid with a thick paste. They will have to return to the siding'

Raoul then had to find another engine to drag the train back, screeching all the way as it was dragged, to the sidings. Eventually he found one just fired up and between one pulling and one pushing, the screeching train was pushed back down the track. Colonel Lammerding was informed and sent a message to OKW that the train could not be moved due sabotage. He then ordered all the men, trucks and tanks off the train into a marshalling area outside Montauban.

Terri saw what was happening, the whole town could

hear what was happening and Yvette wondered what on earth was happening to Wolfie and Wilhelm.

Lammerding then issued orders for the *Das Reich* to refuel everything and set out on the road north.

The Infamous March of the *Das Reich* to Normandy had begun.

Terri was in trouble. Yvette went over to see her.

'What's up?

'it's my younger brother Alain; he shot a German soldier and now the Gestapo are looking for him.

'Oh fuck,' said Yvette, 'just when they were all leaving us. How stupid. What happened?'

'He and his girlfriend were drinking wine at her house when a patrol knocked on the door; it was past curfew hour, and he was not supposed to be there. It was the Gestapo officer called Ernst and he asked why he wasn't Alain away on the service du travail and where had he been hiding. Alain was terrified; he panicked; this was the first time he had been interrogated by the Boches. He gave the excuse that he had been helping on his cousin's farm but under further questioning his story didn't hold up. So, he was ordered to follow Ernst to Gestapo headquarters. His girlfriend told him not to do anything stupid. Ernst poked his gun in Alain's back and told him to move. Outside her house all was going ok but when the officer tried to handcuff him, then Alain reacted; he is a big boy for his age, and he turned and knocked the German flat on the floor; the gun fell, Alain picked it up and shot him dead in the street. Unfortunately, although the rest of the patrol had moved on to the next street, as they weren't expecting trouble from teenagers, they heard the shot and ran back. All the adjoining streets were blocked off and Alain was caught, beaten up then taken away to hotel de Vezin, 3 Faubourg du Moustier."

"You know that's where the torture chambers are' said Yvette, "Wolfie told me that. Maybe you should get your resistance friends to help release him?"

"Maybe you can ask Wolfie for a favour to get him out, just spread your legs in return!' replied Terri, clearly angry and very upset. Yvette ignored the barbed cruel jibe.

'Wolfie has gone, he and his regiment, left yesterday for Normandie; anyway, the *Das Reich* detested the Gestapo as much as we do, they were regarded as crooks and cowards, not soldiers who fight proper battles' said Yvette. 'Look, the soldiers left behind are third rate, it shouldn't be difficult for a well-armed maquis gang to get him and other prisoner's out of that place'.

'They will arrest us all now', said Terri. 'So maybe you are right, we have to strike first. They will either torture him to death or shoot him, there are no transports left running from here anymore'

'Did you say the officer was called Ernst? If so that's the same man who arrested and deported Pascal. It sounds like a good judgement to me,' said Yvette.

'No, that officer who sent Pascal away was called Trascal. But killing anyone of the breed is the same thing,' said Terri.

Yvette decided to visit Raoul in the signal box on the way home. There was no German guard outside anymore.

'Hello' said Hans and nodded to Raoul who was busy working on a big map.

Raoul looked up; 'Hi Yvette, what brings you here?'

'I'm just on my way home, my friend Terri has a disaster because her younger brother shot the Gestapo officer and is in custody'

"Good for him' voiced Hans, 'We don't need those bully boys to help us win the war.'

"I am so sorry,' said Raoul; if they have got him there is not much hope; he will be executed."

'But he is only fourteen years old, surely it can be regarded as an accident?' said Yvette.

'No, that won't wash with the Gestapo, what do you think Hans?' asked Raoul.

'Well, the Gestapo that remain are pretty much the base units, and they will be leaving soon as they fear reprisals from the maquis, so your friend should ask for a meeting and negotiate with them,' said Hans.

'How can you negotiate with those thugs?' asked Yvette.

'Bribe them. They need money to help them escape from here. It might be a large sum; on the other hand, if the bribe is mixed in with threat of death it may work. They know that the Allies will be here sooner or later so they will be keen to save their own skin, only human nature. You just need to be forceful with them'

"Raoul, what do you think? Asked Yvette. 'It could work, but you will need a good negotiator. Someone used to dealing with them.'

'Will you help?' asked Yvette.

'No way can I be involved, talk to Rudi at Café Flaubert. He may be able to suggest someone." Said Raoul

"Thanks Raoul, by the way what are you doing?'

'I have been told to organise rail transport for some of the *Das Reich* regiments from Périgord to Normandy, apparently Périgord marshalling yards are in good shape and have not been disrupted by bombing as much as Poitiers'

'So, they will march on the roads from here to there and the Germans have found flat cars and carriages to take at least a quarter of the division onwards. They will be alright until they cross the Loire, then the allied aircraft will get them,' said Raoul with a smile'.

Rudi was busy in his cellar uncovering wines hidden behind a wall bricked up since the war began. Yvette went down the steps to talk to him.

'Hi Rudi, I can see you're busy. I just want some help please. Do you know someone who could negotiate with the Germans to realise one of the young boys arrested on a murder charge?'

'Ah yes, I heard about that. It was the brother of the Terri girl. Sad. Stupid boy. Sadly, my best contact is busy setting up roadblocks on bridges across the Dordogne, like at Sarlat. He would have done a good job for you but there is no one else around here and its imperative that any negotiator starts as quickly as possible before they shoot him.' Said Rudi.

Yvette said nothing.

'Maybe Raoul at the signal box will do it,' Said Rudi.

Yvette snorted and said nothing.

'Why don't you ask that English agent, what's his

Gerald Glyn Woolley

name, oh yes, Claud, the one hiding at the farm of Madam le Grange' with his pretty assistant

Startled at the comment Yvette said, 'I didn't know about him, what's he doing here, how long has he been here? an English spy is nearby?'

"Aha, that friend of yours Terri told me. I don't know how she knows, maybe Madam's sons in the abattoir, Terri is very friendly with them. And sometimes they can be a little indiscreet'.

Then Yvette dropped the bombshell. "Rudi, you can do it for them. You knew my father well and he went off to war to defend us. He is, we believe, still a prisoner in Germany. Nothing would give him greater pleasure than to know that Rudi did something in the resistance. Please, please, Rudi. You speak German. I can help you collect the money needed for the bribe.

Rudi gulped and said 'Me, I don't know how to deal with this'

'But you know how to barter, because you do that every day for the café, the bread, the coffee, everything that you sell in the café you have bought from someone maybe on the black market, and I am sure you know how to strike a bargain' replied Yvette.

Rudi said nothing for a few moments. Then, with a sigh, said 'ok ask Terri to come to me.'

Fifty-One

ESCAPE TO THE COUNTRY

Pascal and Hugo were running out into the fields around Poitiers. They were also running out of strength; they were desperately hungry. They were running through fields now, alongside the main road to Limoges, and up over the plateau. They spotted an orchard and stopped to pick some apples which helped stay the hole in their belly's a bit. What they needed was proper food, bread at least. They were working their way down the D741 which ran to the west of the N10 on which they could the rumble of heavy traffic. "I reckon its 150K to Limoges' said Pascal; Hugo agreed and added 'we must find some transport, even a horse or donkey will do. It's too far to Limoges and anyway we will be climbing up some 1000 metres into the uplands of the Correze through the forests so it will be hard going on foot.'

The sun was hot. They lay under the apple trees and rested. They dozed in the sunshine. "come on, rouse yourself Hugo, we have to find somewhere to sleep before nightfall. The long afternoon melted into the long evening. They walked for two hours until the summer light was dimming. They spotted a light in the distance. It was a farm. They knocked on the door, a dog barked very loudly, and an old lady opened it. "Who are you? She demanded. 'we are escaped prisoners of war, said Pascal, looking for somewhere to sleep'. She eyed them suspiciously. Then a man's voice could be heard in the background demanding to know who was there. Then he came to the door with the dog on a leash and a shotgun crooked over his arm. Pascal told how they were being transported but escaped from the train when it was bombed, that he and his friend were going home to Montauban. "That's a long way', said the old man.'

Are there Germans here? Asked Pascal. 'No, around here is ruled by the maquis' replied the old man. 'But the Germans have a nasty habit of turning up when you least expect them'. He added, 'but come inside.' Madam had just finished making some onion soup; it smelled so good. They sat down at the kitchen table, and she ladled out a creamy white onion soup, with bread. 'Eat very slowly, digest every morsel, do not rush. 'We haven't eaten for days, and we must get our stomachs gently used to good food,' said Pascal to Hugo.

'Now start at the very beginning' said the old man, still wary of them and with the shotgun on the table near him. So, Hugo and Pascal told their stories from the very beginning, until late in the evening and the candlelight assumed greater and greater brightness as the world went dark. The old man, whom his wife called Dennis, showed them to the barn where the beds of hay just beckoned to them to lie down and sleep, just sleep; and like a drug washing over them they both slept instantly and heavily.

JUNE. 9ᵀᴴ 1944

Terri and Yvette sat down with Rudi in the café to plan his meeting with Ernst, the Gestapo chief now de facto after his boss was shot by Alain.

'Here you have 10,000 francs, courtesy. Of the resistance. Bribe money. Express regret, exude sympathy, and play on the future', said Terri. I thought I might come with you but that could compromise the meeting. Better on your own. Good luck.'

Rudi carried two bottles of very excellent cognac in a small bag and walked up the town to the Gestapo headquarters at the Hotel de Vezin. Two soldiers challenged him as he approached.

'I am here to see captain Ernst on an important matter, please announce me.'

One of the soldiers spoke to the corporal inside; 'the café owner, Rudi, is here to see the captain'

'Search him and bring him inside," said the corporal. Rudi was patted down and searched. They saw the cognac and smiled.

'Not for you, but you are welcome at the café for a free beer any time,' said Rudi.

They showed him into a front room of the hotel, now one of the offices, and bade him wait.

An overplump German orderly in field grey uniform two sizes too big for her entered the room, forage cap slanted well down, with a tray on which were two glasses and a carafe; she was indeed badly dressed and was averagely ugly. She looked evil, didn't say a word but looked disparagingly at Rudi as if he was some low life from the gutter. Rudi shrugged it off. After four years of war, it was nothing to get excited about.

After what seemed an interminable period, but actually only half an hour, Captain Ernst strode into the room with that air of arrogance that precedes small people who think themselves important. The corporal accompanied him.

'Rudi, how nice to see you. I trust all is well at the café?' he said.

'Yes, everything is fine, thank you', replied Rudi. Ernst sat down opposite him and poured two glasses of water out, at which juncture Rudi produced the cognac. Ernst's eyes lit up. He was a stocky man, with a square jaw line and small eyes with big eyebrows. His head sat directly on his shoulders, only a short fat neck separating the two. His sallow skin told of liver problems. His hands were small and chubby, but powerful. Rudi didn't want to think how those hands could hurt you. He had a signet ring on his right middle finger, the one you would naturally hit someone with thought Rudi.

'So, what is the meeting for, do you have information on the resistance?' asked Ernst, in perfect French.

'I have information which I can only share with you,' said Rudi. 'It would be better if we were alone'. Ernst's eyes narrowed even further, becoming almost pig like. But he took the bait and asked the corporal to wait outside, then emptied the water out of the glasses back into the jug and refilled them both with a generous portion of cognac.

'Something as important as this for my ears only deserves that we drink a toast, so please tell me. You have my undivided attention,' he said smiling weakly, thinly in a whinny voice.

'You are in grave danger' said Rudi. 'I overheard six men in the café discussing how they were going to kill you. You are on the hit list of the maquis.'

'We are all in danger, but I have soldiers to guard me so 'poof' to their threats' said Ernst, 'it's a ridiculous suggestion, now what did you really want to tell me? he asked.

'I am serious, there will be two thousand maquis descending on the town tomorrow with the express objective of taking over the town and killing all the Germans here. The first target will be Gestapo headquarters and your head on a pike. I am offering you a way out. No one has to die. We will all win, or we will all lose, I can guarantee your protection and escape.'

Ernst laughed loudly; 'I don't believe what I am hearing; are you threatening me? That's not a good start monsieur Rudi. We still have a well-armed garrison here and can hold out until reinforcements come. How can you guarantee my safety? The maquis are brigands and terrorists; one can't negotiate with them'

Rudi opened a pack of American Marlborough cigarettes, took one and lit it slowly with his lighter. He saw Ernst's eyes opening wide. With a smile he offered Ernst one and gave him a light. Ernst puffed gratefully. Cigarettes were a currency, in short supply in the German army; and American ones were prized. He was about to ask how Rudi had got them but then Rudi broke his thoughts.

'Ernst, let me put myself in your position. No-one is coming to help you. The Americans are already landing on the Cote–d'Azur, The *Das Reich* will be mincemeat in Normandy, if they get that far, once in range of the Allied air force north of the Loire they will be chopped to pieces. My guarantee is as follows; release the boy Alain in the cells, and the maquis won't harm you. They will ensure your escape.' With that Rudi put the 10,000 francs on the desk. Ernst's eyes lit up.

'No one has to know' said Rudi, 'this is between you and me and with the money you can buy your way back home, however I would recommend going to Spain. The Pyrenees are not far away and someone of your strength and good condition can easily cross there in summer'.

Ernst was flattered. He was far from being in any condition to reach the Pyrenees let alone cross them, but valour got the better of him. He knew in, facing reality, that this outpost in Montauban was doomed. He didn't care about the gestapo officer that had been shot, it was his own skin he needed to save now.

'Ernst was thinking, then said 'Look, I just can't release him, questions will be asked.' By now they had half -finished the bottle of brandy. Rudi put the second one on the desk, together with the remaining cigarettes and said, 'You don't have to release him, just let him escape.'

So that night Alain's cell door was left unlocked. He thought it was a trick and if he tried to escape, he would be shot. But Terri had got word to him via the jailer and at midnight he walked out into the cool night air. Terri was outside to greet him. 'You look terrible Alain, what did they do to you? Your face is all cut up.'

"You should see my back where they beat me' he replied. 'But how did you get me out?"

'You have Rudi from the café Flaubert and Yvette to thank, come on, let's go' she said.

The next morning the maquis entered the town. The gestapo building was surrounded. Captain Ernst was nowhere to be seen. Rudi opened the café with free drinks all round. Reprisals started with the collaborators, despite the protestations of Terri and Yvette, who were not unaccustomed to some minor collaboration themselves, but heads of girls who were known to have regularly slept with Germans were shaved in the square, crying, and squealing as the scissors chopped roughly through their locks. Yves started playing with a discarded German rifle until Yvette took it off him. The signal box was quiet,

Fifty-Two

SALVATION

THE FARM

Pascal and Hugo woke late after a long sleep. They were given bread and coffee. Mid-morning the old man said 'we have guests coming, don't worry, they are French not German."

Outside an open top wagon arrived with at least 20 heavily armed men in it. They all got out and 4 came into the farmhouse.

'Bonjour', said the tall man, the leader. "My name is Andre Malraux and I command the maquis in this area. Who are you?'

Pascal and Hugo told their story again, how they were part of Sylvia's band and how they got here. Andre was satisfied then said 'there is a German army heading this way from Montauban en-route to Normandy. Our job is to stop them, harass them, delay them. But you shouldn't move from here or you will be caught. You will be all-right if you don't leave here. Stay put and help the old man with the farm. The roads are too dangerous. We don't know their exact route yet, they will probably split their columns into three, heavy artillery, one way, tanks one way, soldiers another way'

'Wow' said Pascal 'who would bring an army across these mountains, they would have to cross the escarpment south and west of Limoges. It's not tank friendly country'

'That's what we are counting on,' said Andre. 'Then we can snipe at them and block bridges and roads, you two should seriously lie low and stay here. The army will pass through in a week.'

"In my view' said Hugo 'you have no chance trying to fight a fighting army the size and power of the *Das Reich*, it would be suicide.'

'That's right' said Pascal, I saw them in Montauban, and they are formidable.'

Andre smiled; 'we have to teach the Bosch a lesson. Too many French men and women have suffered' With that, the famous Andre Malraux left to go fight the Bosch.

MONTAUBAN

Back in Montauban, the town was quiet. Raoul and Hans sat drinking coffee and watched the silent sidings and signal levers not believing that things were getting back to normal. There were no train services due to the tracks both north and south having been blown up by the maquis. Ironically, with the departure of the Germans there were no gangers or repair men to replace the broken rails. The town was cut off. Food was now non existant.

'So, Hans, what will you do now? Said Raoul. 'Ach,

I will stay here until the Americans come, there is no Germany left to go bk to. Maybe I will be a prisoner of war for a time, or maybe let go. The future is not mine to hold'

'Maybe you can stay and get a job here on the railway, I will vouch for you,' said Raoul.

At the farm Jenny was busy clearing up signals traffic. She had not heard from Claude with no mobile tracker vehicles to trace their signals Jenny clattered away on the ether reporting the news as much as they knew. Lyons, the major hub of Gestapo control would not be liberated for another two months, when American tanks rolled in on September 3rd. However, Jenny had it on good authority from the Maquis that another German column was heading back to reinforce Montauban from Toulouse. As an old man once said 'the Germans have a nasty habit of returning"

Yvette and Terri couldn't believe their eyes when they heard the rumbling of heavy armour coming from the direction of Toulouse. Everyone ran around in panic and Rudi hid his fine wines again. Jenny sent an urgent message to Buckmaster announcing the arrival of an unknown German column. No known details of strength or regiment. Nobody believed it could be any more than a splinter group.

Terri urgently requested information from the maquis cell in Toulouse. There was none. This was a complete surprise and even Yves was scared. They had got used to living with the *Das Reich*, but unknowns could be worse. Rumours circulated that this could be an Italian force or a vengeful Vichy French contingent, even worse. Terri sent Yves home with a big hare for the pot and advised everyone to lock their doors.

Raoul asked Hans about the news but even Hans could not find out from his usual contacts. 'Ach, we will just have to wait and see what shows up' he said.

Pascal and Hugo set to work to earn their keep at the farm, clearing the scrub, finding some old paint to renovate the farmhouse with and generally, in the circumstances, relaxing and getting their strength back. They had made their way from Poitier down back roads towards Pehrilhac and stopped at a Farm outside Cieux, just off the Route de Blond in the Haute-Vienne. The farm was called Ecurie de Blond and was in the triangle of the three roads, the N147 Limoges to Bellac and Poitiers to the east, the D675 to the west and the N141 to the south. A quiet and tranquil farmland and forests. They begged the farmer for some bread and were shown into the kitchen where madam was cooking. The smell of the stew was wonderful. The famer was suspicious to start with but after they told their stories both husband and wife made them welcome. This was a very quiet part of France with little eventful happenings and few Germans. The farmer asked Pascal to chop wood for the range. Pascal was astonished at how weak his arm muscles were, lifting a log required a painful big effort. Hugo was even worse, being a big guy, he had lost even more weight and energy. They both hated to think how quickly they would have gone downhill if they had been sent to a camp.

10TH JUNE 1944

It was another hot day. The few remaining animals on the farm sought shelter under the trees and Pascal and Hugo were busy pumping water from the well and filling the troughs. Towards mid-day they heard armoured vehicles in the distance followed by gunshots and later constant small arms firing. Pascal asked the old man what was going on. He had heard from a neighbour that the Germans were attacking a small village five miles away called Oradour-sur-Glane, situated on a hill twenty-five miles west from Limoges. "The river Glane runs through Oradour, but it's hardly a little brook let alone a river,' said the old man.

"What are the Germans doing up here in the Haut-Vienne' asked Pascal. "There are no military targets here, is there a battle with the maquis perhaps?'

"je ne sais pas' the old Farmer replied. But added 'yesterday there was a huge German army coming up the D675 towards Bellac. No one knows where it is going. Very difficult terrain for an army to cross, small roads, lots of hills and its hot' he said. I will ask my neighbour tonight. Best to stay quiet and away from any roads'

With that Pascal and Hugo continued to fork the hay into the field for the two cows, a pony, and a donkey. At least the chickens were busy clucking away producing lots of eggs which madam made delicious omelettes, seasoned with herbs and spices for lunch. The afternoon passed quietly, madam cooked a big chicken for supper and their neighbours joined them, a young couple from Paris who had settled here before the war, glad to be away from the war-ravaged city.

They were good company, very excited that the war was coming to an end, with big plans for their small farm and to raise their children there. With that she announced that she had just become pregnant, so a bottle of champagne was brought up from the cellar and many toasts were drunk followed by copious quantities of red wine. The chicken was superb, soft, and full of flavour. Pascal finally asked the question about the earlier events of the day.

The young man called Armand replied. "There was a massacre at Oradour, 650 men women and children slaughtered by a regiment of the *Das Reich* division, we heard there were only three survivors."

"Why, why, why, how can that be true? retorted Hugo, clearly very affected by the news. "well,' continued Armand, I have it on good authority from the maquis and also the bishop of Tulle, that it is true. The whole village was burnt to the ground, rumours are that people were shepherd into a barn or church and burnt alive.'

'There must be more to this than just that' said Pascal, if this was the real *Das Reich* then no doubt, they would have been on their way to Normandy. What possessed them to divert for this small village?'

Armand continued; I heard a rumour that the maquis captured Tulle and killed at least 64 Germans and badly mutilated the German soldiers including some in the hospital. 60 German prisoners of the maquis were shot. When the *Das Reich* recaptured the town, they sentenced 140 men to death as a reprisal, they hung 99 then ran out of rope so the rest were sent to Dachau.

Also, a German officer, Major Kamphe was captured

by the maquis and never seen again. The maquis either shot or hung him; so, the Germans had enough of the maquis and decided to make an example, a big example like Oradour. Innocent people paid the price for the adventurism of the maquis. I heard last night that even Andre Malraux told all maquis groups to stand down; no more killing of German soldiers; let them pass; let them go to Normandy; and to let the Americans deal with the *Das Reich* in Normandy'

Tulle and Oradour-sur- Glane was too big a price to pay, Pascal and Hugo were numb. 'I don't believe it' said Pascal 'why do we self-destruct like this with the war ending? Seems to me even though I hate the Germans they were fairly modest in their right to execute partisans.' All of this had been going on down in the South while they were quietly working on the farm, rebuilding life and all the while life was being destroyed.

'I wonder how the Germans have left Montauban, what destruction and deaths have occurred there?' said Pascal, suddenly thinking of his parents and moreover of Yvette. 'As soon as we are strong enough in another few days or a week we must go.'

'You must be very careful, it's a long way to walk and there's still much danger from Vichy police and soldiers. They are worse than the Germans. One day we will get our revenge on them,' said Armand.

The next day the sound of tanks clanging and squealing as they rounded the bends on the main N147 to the east and direction Poitiers could be clearly heard. And the dust raised from the dry roads ballooned up into the sky and sat there, an unwelcome cloud that covered the already dusty hedgerows and grassy fields so that they looked like a sprinkling of talcum powder. It went on all day. 'How lucky we were to escape Poitiers' said Hugo. 'It must be a huge army. Where have the Germans got that amount of resource from' replied Pascal.

Holocaust Village Oradour Sur Glane

MONTAUBAN

Yvette was struggling with her pregnancy. The baby didn't feel right. The midwife said it was too early to tell. 'After all, you are barely six months' she said. 'But I will come and massage you every day, after all there is not much else for me to do, and I live around the corner.'

Terri came often as well to see her and to share the news. By now the threat from the southwest had not amounted to anything; 'it was a false alarm really' she said. 'this column from turned out to be a few broken half- tracks making enough noise to sound like tanks, displaced Italian soldiers, some disillusioned Vichy soldiers from north Africa and about six actual Germans. The local maquis ambushed them and after some fierce but hopeless fighting they gave up and returned east to Negrepelisse in the Tarn. Now our job is to hunt down the collaborators and try and rebuild our lives. It's the middle of July and soon the allies will be breaking through to Paris, we hope. By the way, Pascal's father came to see me, his wife is not so well. She needs penicillin so I have stolen some from the hospital to help her. It's only an infection and will clear up soon. I must ask my cousin in the Pyrenees if he can spare some food, a lamb or two or even an old sheep or goat would help our hunger. There's only so much meat on the rabbits we shoot and now that the Germans have gone everybody has got out their old shotguns and have begun scouring the fields. All the big hares went first then the rabbits'

'If only we could get the cows in milk again' said

Yvette, 'that would be nourishment especially for the baby inside me.'

Terri had become very attached to Yvette and her family, brought her potatoes and other vegetable's.

During one visit Yvette asked her how she had become involved in the resistance

'Well, said Terri, many years ago when the Germans first arrived, they were not very courteous, or professional, not like they have been when *Das Reich* came. But there were still some dances allowed, because we were in the Free Zone. At one dance where the whole town attended, there was one big fat German who insisted on having a dance with me. I refused, he got angry and pushed me down with a kick in my butt in front of the whole assembly. I fell to the floor and all the Germans laughed, some French pigs as well. I was only eighteen. I was humiliated. There is nothing worse for a young girl than being humiliated. So, I decided never to go to a dance again and I spoke to Rudi about what to do because I was angry against the Germans; he suggested that I speak to Alaine, who was getting resistance organised in our area.'

'Wasn't that dangerous?'

'Yes of course, any association with the resistance was forbidden.'

'But you did it anyway'

'Yes, but when you have a burning desire that won't go away, you are driven. It's part of the human condition to have a desire and wanting to be absorbed into something that is bigger than me. A desire unfulfilled will never be satisfied. I learnt that the deepest desire was to know

I counted for something, to know that I mattered for myself'

'What was your role?' asked Yvette.

'I was running errands; my brothers were still at school but soon left to join the maquis to avoid the forced work in Germany. Simple errands, Rudi at the café was our 'post-box' where we left and picked up messages. it was simple but fulfilling to know I was contributing. It became more serious with helping at storing arms and attending le parachutage'

'Wow, I wish I was as brave as you Terri.'

'Well, you became brave without knowing it; remember the night we spoked the grease boxes of the flat cars with grinding paste; under the nose of the Germans in the thunderstorm, that was brave.

It was a big mistake of the Germans to assume that such a night didn't need a doubling of the guard.

And as Napoleon said, never interrupt your enemy when he is making a mistake.!'

Gradually word filtered down from the Correze about the shoot up and the death of Claude. It eventually came to madam La Grange who called Jenny to her in the kitchen.

'I have bad news, Claude is dead. He was shot driving a car while escorting a British agent who was captured; there was also a third person, a Frenchman who escaped. He was the one to tell us the news'

Jenny sat down at the table with tears in her eyes slowly running down her cheeks. Madam made her a big coffee with an even bigger slug of brandy in it.

'I told him it was risky, a mission impossible. He

always said our best asset as agents was luck. and I knew his luck would run out if he went on that mission to meet that woman. I only hope it was worth it. But nothing is worth the tragedy of an unnecessary death.'

With that Jenny gave way to big, long and languid sobs, with her head in her hands. She had become very fond of Claude; she felt she knew him more than if she had known him properly. To think that after all the risks they had taken together in the very midst of the *Das Reich,* in the very centre of the lion's den, to be killed outside of the den in an unfamiliar countryside by maybe a lucky shot filled her with burning sadness. She bitterly regretted not having insisted that Claud should not go on the mission.

Madam made her some hot soup and said, 'You know what Jenny, you can't blame yourself, it's a fool's errand to think you were to blame. This is how the cards fell and Claude was doing his job. As I understand it, it was just unfortunate circumstances, bad luck. Cherish his memory and the times you had together. Don't you agree Jenny?'

'Yes, this bloody war'

Eventually she knew she had to transmit the news to Buckmaster at SOE.

Fifty-Three

TWO MONTHS LATER

AUGUST 21, 1944

t was hot. Pascal and Hugo bid goodbye to their hosts. They had heard that two days earlier on August 19th that Paris had been freed from the Germans by General de Gaulle and the Americans. General Dietricht von Choltitz, commander of the German garrison refused an order from Hitler to blow up the city.

"So, said Pascal, it's over, now Paris is liberated it's time for us to go home. The rest of France will be free soon' Hugo applauded that sentiment loudly but asked the young neighbour Armand about the Vichy forces because they were more of a danger where they were going than the Germans.

'I hear that they are fleeing to Germany to be under the protection of the Germans, but Petain is already in free French custody. he will be tried for treason, and I hope he hangs' said Armand.

They were now fully recovered, and madam's cooking

had brought back their strength. They declined madam's offer for them to stay, be part of the family and eventually inherit the farm but thanked her profusely. They set off down south, first on the back of a hay cart and then they hitch hiked along the roads that winded through the famous grain fields, drinking in the smells of the early harvest, resting often and eating the fruit of the orchards until they got to Brive where they waited for a a train service to Montauban.

The train was smelly and overcrowded with women, children, workmen, chickens, a pig and a priest. But no Germans. The barking of the exhaust seemed to sound like a triumphal march and the click clack of the rails a countdown to joy. Arriving at the station filled Pascal's heart with excitement. He took Hugo to Rudi's café and drank coffee and a cognac or two. Pascal didn't want to be too sociable because his return home was on his mind. Then the march out to the farm. They arrived and Pascal was sad at how neglected it all looked; overgrown, broken fences, tiles off the roof. But at least there were still chickens scratching in the dirt. The door was slightly ajar but instead of going in, Pascal paused and let the moment sink in. His mind raced back to the day he was taken away. Then he knocked on the door. A little old lady with her hair tied back in a bun wearing an old patterned full-length dress and blue cardigan with a grease splattered apron on top came to the door; she looked weary and weather-beaten but beneath it all he recognised his mother; she almost collapsed when she saw him.

'Pascal, Is it really you"

'Yes, mama, I have returned, and this is my best friend, Hugo.

'Oh, mon dieu, both of you come in and sit down. I really thought you were dead'

'We came close to death many times, mama. And we saw so much death to last us a lifetime'

With that mama started to cry. Hugo wrapped his strong arms around her frail body in a warm hug and stroked her grey hair.

'Oh Pascal, such bad times, your father died in the spring from tuberculosis. He would have given anything to see you here again. And what little money we had, I have used up and was on the point of selling the farm'

With that she wept intensely, the tears rolling down her brown sunken cheeks.

'Oh mama, no one is going to take the farm away from you. We are here no to rebuild it up. Hugo has no family left, they have all perished, and has nowhere to go. He is my brother now and together we will make the farm strong and make our lives here.

'Mama's crying eased, and she hugged Pascal tightly.

'Don't ever go away again, please never leave me again, I wouldn't bear it'

'Hey, don't worry mama. We are here now, and you are safe with us. We will make some supper. I will collect some eggs.'

Yvette was having a bad time with the pregnancy. Most days she just lay in bed sweating. Her mother plied her with cold drinks and constantly mopped her brow. Yves was being a nuisance, playing with friends and making too much noise. His mother told him to play in the street. So, he went to see Terri and told her about Yvette. She said she would come to the house straight away and when she arrived, she was appalled to see Yvette in bed.

'She has been here for days; she just can't get rid of the pain,' said mama.

'Has the doctor been?'

'yes, he has given her a sedative but says its more than that and has promised to get help from the hospital, also some natural remedies from the flowers in the woods.'

Terri had heard on the grapevine that Pascal had returned. "Oh, mon dieu, I have to get to see him as fast as possible. I can't let him see Yvette without explaining what happened', By now all the bicycles the Germans had confiscated had been released from the lock up cage by the station, some needed tyres and inner tubes but they were stuffed with straw so worked after a fashion. Terri picked one and headed off to the farm. When she got there, Pascal and Hugo were cutting the hay and stacking it.

'Hi Pascal, do you remember me? she asked, puffing and panting after riding so fast and hard.

'Both boys stopped work. "Yes of course Terri, how could I not recognise such a beauty as you! This is my friend Hugo'. Hugo smiled a big smile, and Terri smiled back. Handsome man she thought.

"Pascal, please may we go inside and sit down. I have some important news about Yvette'

"Yes of course, in fact I was going to go and see her today and invite her up to the farm, maybe take the pony for her. It's been a long time'

'Well, I am so glad I caught you' Terri replied as they sat down in the kitchen.

'Let me get you some water,' Said Pascal.

'Well,' Terri began. 'You remember how earlier in the year Yvette was besotted with you and the relationship you had both begun before he was dragged away. She pined after you day and day and was desperate to find out what happened to you. She went to extraordinary lengths with the resistance, I know because I helped her, and with the Germans. But you had disappeared. Then two SS Officers were billeted in her house, well, one actually but they knew each other well. His name was Wolfie, from Alsace and he taught her piano and was very gentlemanly towards her and the entire family. She asked him several times to help find out where you were. No one knew. But then one day he said he might be able to get some information from the Gestapo. She was so happy that you might actually be still alive. So, she gave herself to him as a big thank you.'

'Well, that's not such a terrible thing, we can easily get over that, I am surprised that there was only one escapade with all the other frisky boys around her,' said Pascal. Terri continued.

'Yes, Pascal, but now the baby is about to be borne. And I didn't want you to stumble in on her without an explanation.'

There was silence. Then Hugo said 'time for a cognac I think'

The drink steadied the conversation.

'Pascal, I quite understand if you want nothing more to do with her. You have a new life beginning and a farm to rebuild. I can tell her, and she and her mother will have to bring the baby up themselves. but there will be questions as to who the father is. The town believes it's you. That you fathered the baby. If they find out otherwise, then you know what they do to girls who fraternised with the Germans'

Hugo cleared his throat.

'Look, Pascal' as Terri said we are starting a new life. Why don't we bring this new little new life about to enter the world, into our world? After all, there will be Alsace genes in there and I have always wanted a son' With that he smiled at Terri who returned the smile with a huge hug. Hugo was impressed and infatuated with the attention. 'There has been so much death and destruction that it would be good to regenerate our lives, and as he grows up, we can teach him about the farm, the animals and get him a pony to ride'

'That's a nice thought, but we don't know if it's a girl or a boy yet' said Terri.

'Well, whatever the sex is, it will be a refreshing change to have to worry about a little life and not our own' Replied Hugo.

'You know Hugo, you are such a kind human being that I could marry you myself, said Terri.

They all laughed.

'Ok' said Pascal, 'I will go and see Yvette in the morning. Terri can you be there as well please?

Terri agreed she would be there and so the next day, Pascal and Hugo met Terri outside Yvette's house. They knocked on the door and mama opened it with a bountiful smile and couldn't resist shouting out to Yvette 'darling, Pascal is home'

They trooped up to them bedroom where Yvette lay prone with a pillow under her legs to ease the pain in her abdomen. She was shocked, tearful and happy all in one instance. Mama brought hot coffee and croissants from the baker next door. Yvette sat up in bed.

"Hello, my little cuckoo, here are some flowers from your favourite field at the farm,' said Pascal.

"I am not little or a cuckoo, I am a big fat cow'

'Not at all, you look radiant' with that he kissed her on the check and stroked her belly.

'I have been waiting so long for this moment and have so much to tell you. This is Hugo, my new blood brother. We have been through so much. And so have you, I hear. So, tell us.'

Yvette sighed and began the long history of her search and fallen moment, at which she started crying. "I know I should have trusted in you to come home but you have no idea how lonely I was and Wolfie looked just like you, he reminded me so much of you and I thought that if he could help to bring news of you a little reward was ok, but I didn't know that such a little reward would lead to this'

Too late, Terri put her fingers on her lips because even her mother didn't know that the baby was not Pascal's but now the secret was out.

Her mother stood up and almost shouted at her 'You dirty little bitch, you slept with that German officer who stayed with us?' Yvette began to sob hysterically.

Pascal put his arm around her, Hugo put his arm around mama. What a scene this is thought Terri. Good job Yves isn't here to see it otherwise it would have been a disaster.

Pascal rescued the moment. "Yes, ok you slept with him, but you slept with me first and if I remember the occasion, how can I forget, you were ovulating, I could smell you, so I was the first and the baby is mine.'

Everyone calmed down. Pascal continued. 'When the baby is born you can bring him to live with us at the farm. I will call him Sebastian and if a pretty little girl like you then Fleur. But now we have to make preparations and make sure you are feeding well. Terri, can you get some nutritious food, plenty of vegetables, we have none left. I can bring a scrawny chicken tomorrow and we will go shooting for a deer in the forest. Hugo is a great shot'

Terri was warming to Hugo. He was the most handsome man, big and burly that she had met in a long time.

"Now, what does the doctor say? 'asked Pascal. 'when is the baby due?

"Not such good news, he can't get any drugs, everything has been stolen or is not available. And the baby should arrive in about three weeks, in September. The weather will be cooler.' said mama. 'We will manage, it's not the first baby to come into this world and there are plenty of us here to help'.

Back at the farm over supper Pascal challenged Hugo.

'Don't you think it's a bit of blackmail? why can't she come clean and tell everyone the truth? After all the Germans have gone."

'Look my friend, it's the worst thing she can do. You had a loving relationship with her, and she was only doing

Gerald Glyn Woolley

the right thing in trying to find you. When we were together with Sylvie, you remember Sylvie don't you, well you never spoke of Yvette, so it was you who abandoned her mentally. She never did. She was faithful to you in that way. Now that you are home and trying to rebuild your life, this gives you a head start. No one needs to know the truth. Look where truth has got us over the last five years. We have become immune to truth. My philosophy teacher told me that a belief is true if there exists an appropriate meaning- a fact - to which it corresponds. If there is no such fact, the belief is false. So where does your truth begin? You know this war started with true words: the words took hold and became bad words and that became the truth. The Jews know this only too well. They let the words get out of control and lost the truth they represented. Your world of truth is nothing in comparison. I think you should seize the moment to rebuild your life with me, Yvette, Sebastian, or Fleur and look after your mum. She is the veritable truth if you ask me. And there can be nothing more beautiful than a girl who wants to spend her life with you, whatever the cost'

'Hugo, what school did you go to? I never knew you studied philosophy!'

"Well, to tell you the honest fact, I went to a Jewish school when I was very young. We moved when I was seven to a catholic school. Good job I wasn't brought up Jewish although I remember my teacher saying that Jewism comes through the female side of the Jew, never the male, after all a mother could have had many men so she is the only true vessel to carry the Jewish genes'

'Now you are going too far,' laughed Pascal. "Ok,

I take your point about Yvette- let's have a coup de champagne to celebrate that we are alive and remember dear Papa, and here's to the future'

He poured three glasses from the bottle his mother had found at the back of the cupboard, and they all kissed each other. Yes, said Hugo, and when you marry Yvette you can have more children, this place needs filling up!

Yvette had good days and bad days, but the good days were great. Pascal went into the town and took her out for walks and then found a pony to carry her up to the farm. The old smells came back, and she was so happy. They walked slowly up to the stream and under the trees that still provided moisture for the plants, they picked what remained of the wildflowers of summer and the hazy and fewer hot days flooded happiness over them. Yvette's mother made her a wicker cradle for the baby, Terri brought vegetables and Hugo hid all day in a blackberry bush waiting for the deer to come close enough. He always chose the female deer, the stags were too tough, and when one nuzzled inside the bush, he killed it with one shot. He told the story later that as the doe lay there, a stag came by and looked at it then continued foraging, after all there were plenty more does for him! So, Pascal and Hugo cooked the deer over an open log fire and the nutritious venison meat provided much needed vitamins and energy for Yvette.

LATE AUGUST 1944

Down in the town, life was getting back to normal. The 15th of August was the turning point. The Milice and any remaining Gestapo clerks left the south on the morning of the 19th, Terri's brothers returned from the maquis, prisoners of war were drifting back from Germany and the train tracks to Toulouse had been repaired and the trains had started to run again. Wheat was arriving at the bakery and bread was plentifully available again.

'Maybe we can go and see Father Bernard again in Tulle,' Yves said. 'It would be nice to go on the train again'

'Maybe, but now my place is here with Yvette,' said mama. "Why don't you go off fishing and bring us back some nice trout?'

'I want my bicycle back; they can't find mine in the cycle cage. Maybe someone has stolen it'

'Go and see Raul or Paul, I am sure they will find it for you. The Germans wouldn't have taken it, it would be too small for them'

Yvette was getting better in herself and busying herself making little pyjamas and some swaddling clothes for Sebastian. She liked the name and hoped it would be a boy. Gifts of little hand knitted cardigans began to arrive at the house from well-wishers. The weather was a lot cooler, September had arrived early and what remained of the harvests were being pulled in. It was back breaking work because there were no horses left. Pascal was lucky, he managed to find a few mules and wild donkeys from up in the woods. He shared them out with his other farmer friends. How Hugo worked, like a giant.

SEPTEMBER

It was now late September and the doctor told Yvette that the baby was well positioned and on the way.

'I am so excited; I can't wait to hold him in my arms'. Pascal had warmed to the idea and had made plans for the marriage. He announced that it would be Saturday September 30th.

And so it was. They managed to get Father Bernard down from Tulle to marry them in St Jacques church in Montauban, located in the historic centre and emblem of resistance, it retained an old-fashioned charm and a privileged place in the heart of the townsfolk. Its bell tower pointed to the sky as if showing the way and stood on guard before the road crossing at the Pont Vieux at the quays of Villebourbon on the other side of the Tarn. The civil service was already done the day before.

The church rang the bells with gusto; the first big happy wedding for four years. It was as the whole town attended; Yves was a little page boy, Madam la grange and her sons, Madelaine baked the bread, Terri brought six chickens and she and her brothers together with Rudi formed a resistance guard of honour. Hugo carried Yvette in his big broad arms to the altar. There were wild country flowers woven into her hair like a crown. She looked radiant, big and beautiful. The reception was in Café Flaubert and Rudi splashed the wine and champagne around endlessly. Pascal got drunk; Terri cuddled up to Hugo and they got drunk together. Francois, mother of the bride was very happy but felt a twinge of sadness that her husband Fabrice hadn't yet returned how from

Germany. All the town celebrated; even the fire brigade got their red snub-nosed Renault fire engine running and raced around the town with Yves ringing the bell, until they ran out of petrol and had to push it back to the station. Everyone went to bed very happy. Yvette stayed at her house where she wanted to have the baby; she was not ready to move in with Pascal just yet.

Fifty-Four

SUNDAY OCTOBER 1ST 1944 THE FULL MOON OF LOVE ARISES AGAIN -99% ILLUINATION

During the morning Yvette, after a sleepless night because her room was lit like daylight, felt movement in her belly and an hour later her waters broke. Mama immediately called the doctor and Madelaine next door. It was a difficult birth later that afternoon. Sebastian entered the world at 1630 bawling his little lungs out, all new little fingers and toes, with a plentiful crop of black hair. Mama placed him on Yvette's breast, he immediately latched on and started sucking noisily. Yvette's eyes opened wide with delight, she hugged his little warm body tightly and smiled, beamingly. She was the picture of happiness.

But Yvette was bleeding heavily. The doctor called

for all the gauze in the house and for iodine to sterilise the material. With that they tried to stem the bleeding. Yves cycled post haste up to the farm and asked Pascal to come quickly. He arrived and started mobbing Yvette's brow with a cold flannel. Her big brown eyes looked up at him as she held Sebastian and her smile of satisfaction and happiness melted Pascal's heart.

The doctor examined her carefully.

'I cannot see the place of the bleeding; it is very deep inside.' He used a pair of binoculars to try and see deeper inside and with the aid of a torch

The cervix is torn; I am afraid of an infection.' He kept pressing on the abdomen.

'Open the windows as wide as you can to get more oxygen into the room, that will help.

'You must do something,' said Pascal.

'Yes, I know but the only other solution is to cauterise the wound, but it is too deep to reach. We must pack more gauze or cotton shirts well sterilised against the spot of the bleeding.

Mama was very anxious. She continued to make hot drinks with lots of sugar in for Yvette.

'We must get her to the hospital but the nearest one for an operation is Toulouse; I don't have any drugs or blood transfusion equipment in my surgery.

And her pulse is very high, her heart is beating very fast to try and pump more blood through'

'I am feeling dizzy' said Yvette in a low whisper. Her eyes were anxious and sad.

Mama brought hot and cold cloths alternatively

pressing them against the abdomen. And gave her plenty of water to drink.

"She is losing too much blood,' said the doctor. The only other solution is a hysterectomy in the hospital, but I am afraid she would not survive the journey even though Toulouse is only 50 kilometers, the roads are so rough after all the army tanks'

The doctor then asked everyone to go pick some herbs, Achillia millefolium or yarrow, the pink and white flowers in the meadows and roadsides.

'I once read that that Pliny wrote about his hero Achilles learning the properties of the plant to reduce bleeding from injuries in combat, we call it 'herbe au coupures' in France. It's worth a try, go quick.

The everybody except Mama and Pascal rushed out the door. Mama tried to take Sebastian away from Yvette, but he was happy suckling and the pausing for a nap.

The search team were back withing 30 minutes with a basket of herbs,

'Boil them up and make a paste out of them, then we will push them up against the cervix as fast as we can,' said doctor.

Remarkably this seemed to stem the bleeding a bit but by now Yvette's pulse was hardly discernible. She was lapsing into a coma. Despite her strength and will power, there comes a time when the mind cannot rule the body. The roots she was born with had somehow become twisted and the veins tangled around themselves.

Hugo wrapped his arms around Pascal who didn't

look up from Yvette. Her eyes were fluttering closed. She spoke pleadingly.

'Pascal, I think I am dying; I am so sorry, please look after little Sebastian and bring him up as one of your own. Tell him about me and how I loved him so dearly, how I would have loved just a few more years. I tried my best and I love you enormously. There is no pain except total grief in my heart that I won't see him grow up.' Yvette was fighting hard with all her courage, but courage is useless when nothing is achieved.

Pascal's tough lined face streaming tears. 'My little cuckoo, I can't face an empty nest, hang on and you will soon be ok.

"Pascal, hold me' she whispered. She held Sebastian tightly and Pascal wrapped his arms around both of them.

Mama sent Yves to fetch Father Bernard. He arrived and they all gathered round the bed. Yvette looked peaceful; her skin was losing its lustrous colour, turning ashen. The bed clothes were soaked in blood. Father Bernard recited the rosaries and touched her head with his finger. Then at 9pm on a beautiful autumn day, with the full moon still high in the sky, Yvette, the laughing mischievous happy young girl slipped away from the world.

Mama kissed Sebastian and gently pulled him away from Yvette and wrapped him in his swaddling clothes and fed him with a bottle of warm milk.

Pascal railed at the priest – 'where is this god who lets a young girl die? And he never gave us the chance of saving the baby or the women.'

'Who would you have chosen?'

'The woman, she can always have more babies'

'Maybe in her condition she wasn't able to have more children. You should be honoured that she gave you a being of her own creation and entrusted you to grow him up in her image. She gave you something of her that you never had. Remember the gospel of St John: Greater love has no one than to lay down one's life for ones' friends- or in this case one's children, so that the vine can grow again. She is not dead; she has just gone away, living on the other side of the world, and you will remember the sound of her voice, her laugh, her smell, forever. She is one of the many casualties of war because in normal times we could have saved her in the hospital in Montauban.

The full moon lit up the bed and its wane yellow shadows seemed to be pulling Yvette's spirit up into the sky to live amongst the stars.

Mama howled loudly; Hugo held Pascal tightly. Terri held Yves and they all cried until they could cry no more. A life so full of promise yesterday had changed into emptiness for them all within twenty-four hours.

AFTERMATH

With Yvette's death, the secret of any shame she might have carried with her for sleeping with a German officer passed into the grave with her. The world could only see that Pascal had a son, and such an equivocation would be but a grain of sand lost in the deserts and deceptions of war.

Pascal brought up Sebastian on his farm, putting his whole life into him. He never remarried.

Terri and Hugo were married a month later and moved into the farm with Pascal. Hugo built a log cabin for them. They had three children: Chloe, Rosie and Alfred.

Raul was promoted to area controller of railways for the whole southwest France.

Hans became a train conductor.

Jenny was picked up by SOE, returned to England and received the DSO medal.

Father Bernard built a shrine in his church in Tulles in remembrance of Yvette and family who used to come to stay as children, and for all the casualties of war.

Hans Lammerding was captured by British before serving one last time as general chief of staff to Heinrich Himmler in the east against the Russians on the Vistula.

Most of the 20,000 strong "*Das Reich*' died in the *Falaise Gap* although with the help of the 1ˢᵗ SS division Leibstandarte who helped keep the gap open for a few thousand to escape to Austria where they finally surrendered to the Americans at Linz with 45 officers, 1330 soldiers and 11 tanks. Although the post war trials indicted many of them for murder at Oradour and Tulle, the French dismissed the cases, and none served their sentences.

When Lammerding died peacefully in Bavaria in 1971. Two thousand SS veterans attended his funeral.

Six months later Fabrice returned from Germany, emaciated but alive. He never fully recovered having contracted TB in the camp and died six months later.

A few days later a letter arrived from Germany addressed to Yvette. Inside was a Medallion on a leather chain of St Christopher. It was from Wilhelm saying that Wolfie had died when his tank was hit in the battle of Falaise gap. Wilhelm thought Yvette might like it back

Madam la grange helped buy the abattoir for her two sons.

Madelaine took Yvette's advice and married a local builder. She still kept the secret recipe of her bread locked away though.

Rudi started another café; his café Flaubert was now run by Yves, and Rudi opened Café Flo on the embankment.

Violette Szabo was shot by the SS in Ravensbruck Concentration camp alongside two other SOE female agents on February 5ᵗʰ1945 on Hitlers orders. Her daughter Tania received the George Cross on her behalf from king George VI on December 7ᵗʰ, 1946. She was four years old and wore the pretty dress her mother had bought for her in Paris during Violette's first mission.

The poem "The Life that I have" was composed by Leo Marks for his girlfriend Ruth who died in a plane crash and later given to Violette Szabo as a cryptographic code for SOE agents. And became enshrined in her memory.

The life that I have
Is all that I have
And the life that I have
Is yours
The love that I have
Of the life that I have
Is yours and yours and yours.
A sleep I shall have
A rest I shall have
Yet death will be but a pause
For the peace of my years
In the long green grass
Will be yours and yours and yours.

THE END

Further reading, information, acknowledgements and government sources:
Das Reich – Max Hastings
Fighters in the shadows -Robert Gildea
Deposition 1940-1944 – Leon Werth
SOE and the resistance – Times Obituaries
Suite Francaise – Irene Nemirovsky
Tourist information office Montauban France
Military Museum Caen Normandy Franc

Printed in the United States
by Baker & Taylor Publisher Services